Turning In

More Stories of Brenna and Cassidy

Lara Zielinsky

Supposed Crimes LLC • Matthews, North Carolina

All Rights Reserved
Copyright © 2023 Lara Zielinsky

Published in the United States.

ISBN: 978-1-952150-40-1

Cover art by Somewillwin

Cover design by Geonn Cannon

www.supposedcrimes.com

This book is typeset in Goudy Old Style.

AUTHOR'S NOTE

Brenna and Cassidy were the lead characters in my first novel *Turning Point* and its sequel *Turn for Home*. Both books are available in eBook, paperback and hardback second editions from Supposed Crimes.

Though the two women had gone through quite a lot and were firmly together by the end of the second novel, there were many adjustments yet to be made to bring together their working lives and homes with their sons. I wrote these stories to fill in some of those gaps.

TABLE OF CONTENTS

THE END OF THE BEGINNING

Pinnacle Studios, Los Angeles, California
April 2001

PRINCIPAL SHOOTING for the series finale of *Time Trails*, which would air on the network as a two-hour movie event, had reached its last day. After so many years with the same people and the recent upheaval in her personal life, Brenna Lanigan was unsurprised that she felt, to put it mildly, emotionally wrecked watching the crew move swiftly around her to reset for what would be her final scene as Commander Susan Jakes. She resisted the urge to brush her fingers through her auburn hair which had been sprayed carefully moments ago by Angel from the studio's makeup team.

She sensed movement to her right. Turning her head, her gaze followed Cassidy Hyland as the blonde woman stepped up and onto her mark on the Vortex dais. Though she was relieved to see the woman and wanted to speak, Brenna hesitated when she fully took in the other woman's costume and makeup. The makeup team had given Cassidy a roughed-up appearance with gray smudges around her eyes and cheeks. A thin line slashed across her cheek, marks of a pitched struggle Cassidy's character, Chris Hansen, had endured just before she was found. Her uniform too had been 'distressed' and strategically torn.

Brenna had been off camera but present when those fight scenes were shot three days earlier. And even though she knew it was special effects and a storyline, the sight of the 'battered' woman reminded her of Cassidy's too real recent hospital stay.

Swallowing down her reactions even as she felt her hand flexing with the memory of cradling Cassidy on the floor of her trailer, Brenna lifted her gaze to the other woman's face where she found a reassuring smile.

"Hey," Cassidy said, blue eyes light and full lips lifted at both corners. "I'm fine, you know."

Of course her lover recognized her mood, Brenna fretted and tried again to neutralize her expression. "Makeup's pretty convincing."

"Marks," sounded somewhere behind her and she watched Cassidy roll her shoulders and shift her weight from one foot to the other.

"Hug then a kiss, right?" Brenna asked. They'd rehearsed the scene's final moment both ways.

"Yes. I'm looking forward to it." After adjusting her blonde hair, which hung in a messy and haphazard bun, Cassidy placed her hands behind her back. Her head lifted and her blue gaze found Brenna's once more. She gave a tight nod without a smile, but her eyes were so warm. Brenna felt her cheeks heat and her stomach flutter in response.

We're really going to do this, she thought. *Finally.*

Movement to her left made them both jump, still reluctant to be caught in their real feelings. Their co-star Sean took his place next to Brenna at the console controls. "Hi," the blond man said.

"Hey," she replied.

"You didn't have to stop smiling. Everyone here knows you love her," he said. Then he dipped his head toward the cameramen. "And very shortly the proof will be on tape so everyone out there will know it, too."

"Sound effect," came a gaffer's voice off to the right. "3-2-1." That, Brenna knew, was their cue.

"*I've got a temporal lock,*" Sean said, moving his hands across the status board.

"*Is it – ?*" A gaffer setting off a buzzer cut Brenna off.

"*Vortex active,*" Sean said. "*Coming through.*"

Shifting her gaze from Sean, Brenna inhaled sharply and

swallowed as she reacted to the person who appeared through the swirling rift. "C-Chris!"

Cassidy stepped forward as though she was off-balance and weak. Brenna caught her pitching forward, falling from the dais. Grasping Brenna's arms, Cassidy steadied herself. "I've been trying... months... back to you."

"You're safe." Brenna easily conveyed relief and awe and eased her grip on the other woman. Cassidy straightened, displaying the occasional grimace suggesting things were painful.

"Welcome back, Lieutenant." Sean stepped around the control station toward the two women.

"Thank you." Cassidy shook his hand but then she turned back to Brenna. "Heatherly taunted me with recordings – timelines where you died."

"I – we," Brenna hesitated, wringing her fingers. "I'm glad you're safe."

"We got Heatherly, Chris. It's really over." Sean started to put his hand on Cassidy's shoulder, but pulled it away at the last second. "There's a party in the dining hall when you're ready."

Cassidy and Brenna didn't take their eyes off one another while Sean walked off camera.

"How are you?" Cassidy asked as her gaze searched Brenna's.

Tightly controlling her voice, Brenna sounded brittle. "Why did you leave?"

"I couldn't stand being in conflict with you any longer. Then Heatherly abducted me."

"I didn't realize he had you when we apprehended him on Terra-4."

"You wouldn't have found me," Cassidy said. "I had already escaped."

"He knew that. H–he made it look..." Brenna finished Susan's lines, but once again caught in the memories of Cassidy's real stay in the hospital her voice choked. "like... you were dead."

Cassidy took Brenna's hand. "I'm not dead. I'm here."

Brenna forced a smile. She grasped Cassidy's other hand and that steadied her, acting or not. "Yes. Yes, you are." Her second attempt at a smile came easier.

"Yes, I am." Cassidy concluded their lines, stepped closer and lowered her voice as her character broke protocol and used her commanding officer's first name: "Susan."

Brenna lifted her trembling chin and the woman's eyes darted back and forth, gauging, assessing, pleading. "Chris."

She grasped the blonde by both shoulders, pulled her close,

and hugged her. Heads falling to each other's shoulders, they remained embraced for a long silent moment.

Lifting her head, knowing the kiss was next, Brenna looked up into soft blue eyes and a warm smile. She leaned in, gaze focusing on full pale lips.

"Cut!"

Cassidy squeezed Brenna's shoulder and Cassidy's lips turned down as they both exhaled with real disappointment. Tears had gathered in the corners of Brenna's gray-blue eyes. Brushing the arch of Brenna's cheeks lightly with her thumbs, Cassidy said, "You're going to need to pat carefully before another take." She did dare, however, to kiss the other woman's lips, perhaps especially because she knew it wasn't on camera.

Brenna cleared her throat, stepped back, and dabbed her fingertips at the corners of her eyes. "Damn," she commented at her fingers.

The two women didn't get a moment alone to talk about what had happened. The director, Mike Cutter, walked up. "We're done," he said flatly.

"That's it?" Brenna asked. "We're ending on a hug?"

"It's a powerful hug," he said with false brightness, clearly trying too hard.

Cassidy interpreted his body language, shoulders rounded and head down, and drew the only logical conclusion. "The network nixed the kiss."

"Yes. The rest of the episode and the intercut scenes are allowed only to suggest the story."

Cassidy said nothing to that. What could she say? It was unfair, but it wasn't his fault. He would have filmed it if he could. The man was gay himself. He and his partner had hosted Cassidy and Brenna at their West Hollywood apartment and even a Redondo Beach cabin when they had wanted time together without the paparazzi finding them.

Cassidy knew she and Brenna needed time alone to process much more than the end of the series shoot. This scene had revived real memories for both of them: Mitch's attack on Cassidy back in February. She had been unconscious for much of it, but Brenna's eyes had become a dull gray, a sure sign she was in emotional pain. The same anxiety had filled the woman's gaze at her hospital bedside daily for more than two weeks. She grasped Brenna's hand

and kissed her again. "Let's go."

Continuing to hold her lover's hand, Cassidy stepped off the set and led Brenna around to the back lot and the cast trailers. A tent stringed with lights set up on the grounds beyond the furthest trailer drew their attention in the twilight. From the same direction rose a cacophony of conversation and laughter. Someone in the crowd, however, noticed them coming because a kazoo sounded a rough approximation of the show's theme song.

The kazoo player stepped from the shadows and Cassidy smiled. It was Rich, who portrayed the *Time Trails* medic. "Good evening, ladies." He bent slightly at the waist and took off an imaginary hat to complete the bow. Straightening and giving each of them a warm smile, he turned and gestured to the rest of the crew. "Care to join a few out-of-work actors for a celebratory drink?"

Giving Brenna's shoulder a squeeze before she stepped forward, Cassidy kissed Rich's cheek. "Of course. No press questions and no cameras." Fully dropping their characters to mingle would be good for both of them, she decided.

"Well, the cameras may come out later. But this is just an old-fashioned strike party," Rich agreed.

"Nothing old fashioned about it. I love theater."

The man's brown eyes danced. "Good. You know, I'm writing a play. There's a role you could be perfect for."

"I have no plans at the moment. But we'll have to see."

"Think about it," he said, grasping her hand and passing her forward. She and Brenna walked past him.

A woman of mixed Latin and Black heritage with short dark hair secured in a cloth bandana, Rachelle stepped up to them carrying a tray of plastic champagne flutes. "Finally." She passed out the stemware. "We were wondering if you could lead us one last time, Commander." She grinned, leveling a smile at Brenna. "In a toast."

Cassidy looked around and saw everyone had retrieved a similar champagne flute and were standing silent. No one commented on the shine in Brenna's eyes when Rachelle wrapped her arms around the woman who was, by any definition, the ensemble's lead.

"I think I can do that," Brenna whispered. If her voice sounded a little shaky, no one commented on it.

After tracing a line with her finger through the condensation, Brenna lifted her drink and her voice. "Five years ago we all had no idea what the hell we'd stepped into. 'Interesting' doesn't quite begin to cover the journey we've been on, but I am proud to have been on it with each and every one of you. Cheers!"

A chorus of "Cheers!" answered. Cassidy sipped at her champagne as the cast and crew went back to their chatter. Brenna took a step back until their shoulders were aligned.

"Yes?" Cassidy asked from behind the rim of the glass.

"I'd like to get out of our costumes."

"You want to leave now? We just got here."

"Everyone else already changed," Brenna said. "I feel a little out of place. And I know your costume's even more uncomfortable than mine."

Cassidy marveled again how much could change in less than a year. Last September she had been desperately hoping for the woman next to her to give her so much as the time of day. Now Brenna was her loving and attentive partner. Despite this being her first same-sex relationship – a drunken college groping not withstanding – it felt far more reciprocal than any of her previous relationships. Finishing her champagne, Cassidy put the empty plastic flute down. "Are you planning to help me out of it?" she asked, then offered a teasing smile.

The older woman's gaze slid over her from head to toe, leaving Cassidy feeling as though she had been warmly caressed. Knowing how Brenna's hands felt on her intimately fueled the ball of heat growing slowly in her stomach.

Throatily, Brenna mused, "I did make the toast already. They shouldn't miss us."

Cassidy leaned forward until she had her lips against Brenna's ear and felt the soft strands of auburn hair tickling her lips. "They might but, frankly, we've been good all day. We deserve a little time to ourselves."

Brenna's palm cupped Cassidy's cheek when they separated. It was easy to tell the older woman's emotions now that Cassidy knew what to look for. Her blue-gray eyes were shaded bluer now that she was relaxed and happy. Brenna's hand slid down Cassidy's shoulder and arm, raising more warmth and tingles, then she interlaced their fingers.

"We do," Brenna agreed in the husky tones that Cassidy had once confessed made her think of smoky jazz clubs.

The woman also knew exactly what her tone did to Cassidy's insides. Looking over her shoulder to see if they were being observed, Cassidy realized the rest of the cast were oblivious, having gone back to their conversations, food, and drinks. She took her lover's hand and led the way back to the graveled path and on to her trailer.

Standing at the bottom of Cassidy's trailer steps, instinct made Brenna to give a quick look around. They were alone, having just left the informal cast party. But she still felt vaguely unsettled by the memory of Cassidy being attacked here just four months ago. Nothing threatened them now. She was openly dating the woman, and yet it was still an unusual feeling to be here, like this, waiting on her lover to change out of costume.

"Are you coming up?" Cassidy's voice drifted out of the trailer.

Brenna moved quickly up the concrete steps and entered the sparsely decorated space. She pulled closed the door and locked it behind her, so they wouldn't be disturbed. Flower arrangements stood on various surfaces. Fans were still sending them every week since Cassidy's injury. She plucked out the note from the nearest one: "We love you." Turning to find Cassidy stood next to a closet at the far end of the trailer, Brenna put the note down.

Her blonde hair was already unpinned and the top of her costume had been pulled off Cassidy's arms and upper body. The trailer lighting harshly illuminated the woman's skin, and Brenna's gaze went to a scar on Cassidy's ribs that would never quite go away.

As always, she felt the urge to soothe, to replace the violence Cassidy had suffered at Mitch's hands with tenderness and love. She cleared her throat drawing the blue-eyed gaze toward her. "Would you like some help with that?"

"Like I could stop you," Cassidy said in a light teasing tone. Her full lips curled upward in the corners and she licked them as she turned. Without the costume's padding and stiffened shape to lift her breasts, Cassidy's figure was less "bombshell" and yet all the more appealing to Brenna.

Too bad the male gaze put that costume together. *She is so much more beautiful like this.*

"I just wanted to be sure. You seemed to have some definite ideas what you wanted to do when we got here." She stepped closer, drawn by the desire she saw in the woman's eyes, which were such a pale blue they almost appeared white, pierced by dilating pupils.

"I'm sure I need you to touch me, Bren."

Cassidy grasped Brenna's hands and placed them on the

costume bunched at her waist. Together they pushed it off her hips. Brenna followed the costume down until she knelt at her lover's feet. Bikini underwear kept Cassidy's modesty, but the thin cotton did not mask the rising scent of arousal. Brenna's nose twitched and she licked her lips, grasping Cassidy's hips once again.

"Sit down, darling."

Cassidy shifted and sat down on a small bench built into the side of the trailer next to the open closet. Brenna soothed her hands over muscled thighs and tugged the costume off Cassidy's legs and feet. Once it was completely off, Brenna stood and placed the costume carefully on its hanger.

"You too," Cassidy said, patting the seam of Brenna's costume.

She looked down into Cassidy's upturned face and cupped the woman's cheek softly as Cassidy's hands settled solidly on her hips.

Brenna lifted her hands to the insignia lapels and separated the Velcro so her jumpsuit loosened across her chest and back. The costume's padded chest had constricted what little chest she had. She inhaled a deep breath and felt the trailer's air conditioning blow against her sweaty skin.

Cassidy's hands tugged the costume to the floor and Brenna hung it next to Cassidy's in the closet. Briefly she wondered if she should make sure it was in her trailer. Then she felt Cassidy's warm palms against her naked waist and she doubted Costuming would care whose trailer it was in, just so long as they could account for it when closing the set.

Cassidy's fingers and palms were spreading wide across her waist and heat pooled in Brenna's center. Turning to face Cassidy once more, Brenna found Cassidy smiling up at her again before Cassidy dropped her gaze and the delightfully maddening feel of fingers across her belly button were replaced by full lips pressing kisses to Brenna's stomach. Brenna pushed Cassidy back and pressed her lips against Cassidy's. The other woman pulled down until Brenna settled onto her lap.

They hugged for an indulgently long time, arms wrapped around one another and breasts sliding together, Filled with delight, Brenna hummed in Cassidy's ear, inhaled her scent, and nibbled gently at the skin where shoulder and throat met. With her tongue she chased the vibrations of a moan working its way up Cassidy's throat.

The moan finally resolved into words. "Uh-o-mm-*God!*"

Cassidy's hands worked similar magic on Brenna's skin,

circling her hips, sliding warmly up her back, digging in when Cassidy moaned into her mouth.

Leaning back, Brenna chuckled and cupped the back of Cassidy's head with one hand. She stroked the woman's throbbing pulse point, debating whether to suck or nibble. Should she mark her or simply indulge in the feel of the soft skin. They had no more cameras to worry about. Pinnacle publicity had ended with the series. They were free to appear in any way they desired. She leaned forward, nibbling on Cassidy's bottom lip. Then, when the soft lips parted, she delved inside the luscious mouth with her tongue. When Cassidy again gasped, Brenna chuckled and curled her fingers into Cassidy's hair, reveling in the flushed woman's appearance. She hugged Cassidy and groaned herself at the delight of their flesh together.

Nipples poked into her chest and drew her attention away from the delights of nibbling Cassidy's jaw. Within the security of Cassidy's arms making sure she didn't fall, Brenna leaned further back, met blue eyes, and smirked. She cupped one soft mass and lifted it, holding Cassidy's gaze the entire time. Fondling, squeezing, then briefly toying with the nipple, she broke the gaze and settled her lips upon the woman's breast, teasing the nipple hard with her tongue and teeth.

"Oh, mmm, hmm." Cassidy's hands kneaded the muscles of her back. Arousal warmed and soaked Brenna's center as she felt the woman's deep love through her touch. She stopped pulling at Cassidy's breast long enough to offer up a throaty moan of her own.

When the sharpest rush receded and she could think clearly a moment, Brenna returned her attention to Cassidy's chest. She covered the right with her palm and drew the other hardened tip into her mouth, flicking it with her tongue then biting down.

Cassidy gasped. Her hands on Brenna's back flexed then slid down, clasping Brenna's ass tightly against her as she canted her hips. The heat from Cassidy's center felt scorching now against the soft skin of Brenna's belly. She trailed her hand from Cassidy's neck down the woman's side, reveling in the occasional muscle quivers from the light tickle. Insinuating her hand between their bodies, she soothed the back of her knuckles against Cassidy's belly before turning her palm and sliding her fingers under the waistband of the woman's underwear.

Finding fine hairs and damp folds, Brenna pulled at the nipple in her mouth while she pushed one finger further down and curled it inside her lover. The woman's clit pulsed against the side of her finger. She rubbed it more intentionally, eliciting another gasp.

"You're so wet." She abandoned the woman's breast and claimed her mouth in a kiss while she continued to move her finger inside Cassidy. Just the one digit was held snug in sublime heat and wetness. She swallowed Cassidy's gasps and moans until she couldn't wait any longer to taste her. She broke their kiss and removed her finger, placing the digit in her mouth. The subtle flavor only made her crave more. "I need to taste you."

She slid from Cassidy's grasp though the woman's fingers slid into her hair, nails faintly raking through Brenna's shoulder-length locks. Between Cassidy's legs, Brenna tugged at the underwear. Cassidy lifted her hips, quickly casting modesty aside.

"Lean back." Brenna cupped Cassidy's hips and ass as she moved and lifted as Cassidy eased back, holding herself up onto her elbow. Brenna lifted one long leg over her shoulder and kissed the woman's softly muscled inner thigh.

Cassidy's swollen clit showed proudly. Brenna lightly caressed it with her fingers before pressing two fingers inside her lover. Kissing the swollen nerve bundle, she delighted in Cassidy's tightening grip in her hair and the moans of pleasure tumbling from her lips. The motion of her fingers was slowed by the squeezing of her lover's inner muscles. Sliding her tongue around Cassidy's clit, she pulled it between her lips.

Listening to Cassidy's moans, Brenna guided her lover closer and closer to orgasm. Long luxurious moments passed while Brenna indulged in the feel, sound, and taste of her lover gradually coming undone. When Cassidy came, Brenna's name falling from her lips, liquid pleasure dripped onto Brenna's palm. She rubbed the heel of her hand against Cassidy's mound until the blonde came again. Removing her fingers, Brenna licked and sucked until Cassidy's clutching at her head became tired caresses.

She pressed a kiss to Cassidy's folds, then her belly, and finally, slowly, she returned to her feet, caressing Cassidy's sweat-soaked curves. Cupping Cassidy's cheek she pressed a tender kiss to each corner of the blonde's lips before letting her taste herself on Brenna's tongue.

At last pulling back, she drank in the sight of Cassidy akimbo on the bench. A rosy glow suffused the younger woman's usually pale skin. Her chest rose and fell deeply, nipples still peaked. Full lips parted around each breath. Moved by the beauty, she murmured, "I love you."

"Bren." Cassidy's voice was worn and soft. She lifted a hand which Brenna caught. She blinked dazedly. "What you do to me... wonderful." She licked her lips. "When I can move, we're going home where I will show you just how deeply I love you, too."

When they emerged from Cassidy's trailer, Brenna wore a borrowed T-shirt and shorts despite the cool night air. Cassidy's pants would have been too long since Cassidy's height was nearly all in her legs.

"You need some pants?" Cassidy asked. Brenna shook her head. As they returned to the walk which led back around the studio buildings, their embrace slipped and she entwined their fingers. She marveled again at how naturally they moved together.

Noise and voices drew her attention. The tent gathering had not yet broken up.

"Cass! Bren!" It was Rich, carrying a full-size DSLR camera. Cast members were hugging and chatting, exchanging details to meet up later. Cassidy knew while they might run into one another during sound rerecording, it wasn't expected they would all be together like this again.

Phones to record details were in turned used to record group selfies. Rich coaxed the entire ensemble into several group configurations.

Sean was nominated as point man because he planned to remain with the studio, directing episodes of their other series.

Noticing Brenna rubbing the side of her face for a third time, Cassidy grasped her lover's hand and drew her from the crowd. "I'm taking her home," she said to Rachelle. Several people near them laughed and the smiles were fulsome.

Will Chapman stepped forward and Cassidy hesitated. Even with all the mingling and posing, it had seemed like the man was avoiding them. But he was smiling, so she relaxed a little.

"Will," Brenna said.

"Bren," he responded warmly. "We haven't had a chance in the last week to say much."

"I know."

"This series is the first thing I've been involved in beginning to end," he said.

Cassidy nodded. "Same."

"I haven't been many places longer," Brenna said. "What's next for you?" Her tone was interested, but Cassidy couldn't decide if it was for show or genuine.

Their interactions with Will Chapman had been complicated from the very beginning. The man had decided to "help" the two women get together in a rather twisted way involving their roles on the series. In fact, had the writers gone another way, Will's character Raycreek would have been the one to greet Hanssen's return.

"I'm going to visit my sister and my nephew," he said. "Arizona. California's not the place for me."

"You're leaving acting?" Cassidy asked, surprised.

He shrugged. "Maybe. There's community theater pretty much everywhere. I don't think some of us are suited for Hollywood politics. What about you?"

"I'm not sure. Ryan starts kindergarten in the fall and I'd rather be more present for that," Cassidy replied. "But Terry's got a troupe together and Rich is writing plays. They've both asked me to consider working with them."

Will turned to Brenna. "What are you doing next?"

Taking a moment, no doubt to collect her thoughts, Brenna kissed Cassidy's cheek then brushed the spot tenderly with her thumb before turning back to Will. "I have a movie offer, but I have to talk with my partner about whether it's a good idea or not," she answered him.

Cassidy knew that intending for them to plan together showed how Brenna felt about their relationship more than words.

"We haven't discussed a summer vacation," Cassidy said, "for our family." She smiled and squeezed Brenna's hand at her side. Her lover's eyes shifted through gray-blue turbulence before returning to a bright blue. Color warmed the older woman's cheeks and Cassidy felt Brenna squeeze her hand back.

At the same time Cassidy felt the corners of her lips tilt up, Will said, "I'm glad to hear it." He dipped his head. "Take care of each other," he added before briefly touching Brenna's shoulder then Cassidy's arm. Then the women were looking at his back as he walked away into the night, presumably to the parking lot.

Brenna asked, "Would you really come to Ireland with me?"

"Perhaps we can show our sons some sights before you start work on the film in earnest."

"I guess I'd better find out the dates for certain," Brenna said. "So we can plan properly."

Becoming Family

Los Angeles, California
May 2001

RYAN, CASSIDY'S five-year-old son, called out, "Mommy, I need my truck."

Cassidy paused in shredding the lettuce for salad. Looking up across the prep island through the hanging wine glasses and rack, she saw her son sitting among an array of plastic toy cars and trucks in the middle of Brenna's living room floor. "Looks like you have all your trucks and cars there."

"My BIG truck," he replied, small arms spreading wide.

"Your storage truck?" She recalled the collection had a truck-shaped 'suitcase.' "Are you done playing then?"

"Yes." He stood up and tossed the two cars in his hands at his sock-covered feet.

"If the case isn't there with you, how did you get the cars and trucks out here?" she asked.

"Blanket." He pointed to a quilted blanket decorated in primary-colored animal shapes.

She nodded, recalling she had seen James, Brenna's younger son, scoop them into a blanket to clean the living room before. Her son Ryan, quite observant for five years old, must have learned it from watching him. "All right. Put all your cars and trucks in the blanket again and take them back to the room," she said. "Then you can help me with setting the table."

Ryan dropped the quilt on the floor, covering most of the cars and trucks. Between flipping up and down the corners he managed to get most of the toys into the middle of the blanket. Then he picked up one quilt corner. In the process of walking over to pick up another, many of the toys rolled off another side. "No!" he shouted angrily and threw down that corner.

When it looked like the situation would repeat, Cassidy asked, "Would you like some advice or help?"

"No!" His face screwed up in frustrated concentration. Cassidy watched him try again with the corner on the side where the toys had rolled off. "Mommy! Help!" His eyes were glassy with tears and his face red with anger when he looked up at her.

Cassidy couldn't stop working on dinner, knowing her lover Brenna and the woman's teen sons, Thomas and James, would be home any minute. Speaking calmly to Ryan, she said, "Listen to the steps. Pull all the corners into the middle, then you can grab them up together."

Following her advice, Ryan finally had all the quilt corners grasped tightly between both hands. It was too large to pick up off the floor, but he walked his legs around the bundle and did move it out of the living room. Distantly, she heard a clatter and knew she'd have to help him clean it up again before they left to go to their own house later that night.

Ryan, blond hair falling into his eyes, ran into the kitchen and looked up. His beaming smile showed how proud he was. "Mommy, all done."

She smiled warmly. "Very good. The silverware is in that drawer there. How many will you get?"

"Me 'n' you. Two," he said, gesturing between them.

"What about Brenna and Thomas and James? How many?"

"Brenna." Ryan held up one finger on his left hand. "Thomas." He held up one finger on his right hand.

Curious about his thinking, she added herself to that list next. "Mommy."

Ryan looked at his fingers and then pushed up a second finger on his left hand. *Interesting,*

Cassidy thought. "Now James and, finally, add yourself." Ryan finally managed to lift just two more fingers on his right hand, though he struggled a bit to keep it from being all five.

Proudly he stated, "Two and three."

"Two plus three," she corrected. "What does that make all together? Add the numbers."

He looked at his hands intently for several seconds then smiled wide. All the fingers went down on both hands before he threw only his left hand into the air with all five fingers spread wide. "Five!"

She nodded and smiled back at him. "Very good. Now, get the silverware and take it to the table."

Ryan opened the drawer and looked over the front edge. He tried to pull all the forks into his two hands–Brenna had setting for twelve.

"Just five remember," she reminded.

Dropping the forks with a clatter, he then picked up five, one at a time, counting aloud. "One, two, three, four, five."

Watching over her son's progress, Cassidy finished her salad prep, glancing toward the oven where a timer ticked down the last few minutes of the baked herb chicken. The clock there also reported the time as half past five. Brenna had texted her meeting would run a little late, but Thomas and James should have already arrived from school.

Just as she thought about the teenagers, she heard a key in the lock and looked expectantly toward the front foyer. She couldn't see the door from this angle, but she heard the boys talking as they entered.

"They do that march thing every year?" James, the younger of Brenna's two sons, said.

"Yep." Thomas' reply was strained a bit. Once he rounded the wall, Cassidy saw why. His backpack bulged on his shoulder and his arms were full of more bags.

"What's all this?" she asked.

Thomas turned around and his brown eyes took her in with a smile. "Last day," he said. "Had to clean out my gym locker, my class locker, and take home all my projects." He looked down at Ryan holding spoons. "Hey, bud."

"Hi, Thomas," Ryan replied. "Toys?" he asked.

Thomas shook his head. "This is my school stuff."

"Oh." That seemed to make it entirely uninteresting, Cassidy noted. Her son rounded his shoulders and, feet plodding, walked away to finish setting the table. Thomas took his belongings into the bedroom hallway. She heard a door open and close, knowing his room was the last on the end.

James hadn't retreated and instead watched Ryan at his task, so Cassidy studied him. Brenna's younger son was stockier than his brother, and shorter. His hair, though the same dark brown, was in a shaggier sort of cut. She smiled when she saw his hand wrapped around one strap of his backpack–and perpetual paint on his fingers. The backpack also looked considerably less stuffed.

James answered her curiosity. "It was *seniors'* last day," he stressed. "Admin had them all march out through the courtyard while the rest of the school watched. The band played their class song, cheerleaders danced, and the chorus sang the alma mater. Class officers announced the superlatives and they hung a big banner, Class of 2001."

"That does sound neat. Is that why you're so late?" She couldn't recall what her senior class in high school had done. She'd only attended two years of college before she decided acting was what she really wanted to do. She wondered about Brenna's school experience. "You should put all that down and wash up." The oven buzzed behind her. "Dinner's ready."

"One reason. I also asked Thomas to take me by the gallery for a bit." He showed her the color on his fingers. "I'm working on an acrylics project. Where's Mom?"

"Her meeting ran late. She should be here soon though."

"Cool." He reshouldered his backpack and passed Thomas returning to the living room as he went to his own bedroom.

"Anything I can help with?" Thomas asked. Cassidy nodded, lifting the glass baking dish from the oven to the counter. "Please check Ryan set the table correctly. I'm going to pull down the plates and set out the dishes."

He nodded and pushed off the island. She turned away to the cabinets and, between collecting dishes, glassware, and finding the platters and bowls for serving, she listened to the older boy talking with her son.

"Nice job, bud," Thomas said. "You got almost everything in the right place." There was a pause. "Except this spoon goes outside the knife."

The soft clattering of silverware being rearranged reached Cassidy. *He's so good with Ryan.* It hit her for a moment that he wouldn't likely be still around when Ryan started school in the fall.

"Have you given more thought to your college plans?" she

asked, stepping out with the platter of chicken.

"Hmm?" Thomas looked up from where he crouched, sharing a hug with Ryan. "Oh, um, I still want to check into a few programs before I decide."

"Still thinking of something with the outdoors?"

"Yep." Thomas stood up which brought him to her eye level. *A strikingly handsome young man.* She saw a little of his mother's features in the shape of his nose and the set of his eyes, but his tall, slender frame had to be from his father since Brenna was petite, several inches shorter than Cassidy's five-eight. His brown hair and James' were definitely from his mother, the same fine thin strands though without quite as many hints of red.

At the same time James emerged from the bedrooms, there was noise at the door and everyone turned in the dining room to see Brenna Lanigan enter. Dropping her keys in her purse and putting it on a side table, she said, "Sorry I'm late."

"We were just sitting." Cassidy smiled from where she had just been coaxing Ryan into his seat.

James and Thomas had taken their seats. She kissed Ryan's forehead and gestured for him to put his napkin in his lap. Then she walked around the table and greeted her lover at the archway to the dining space. She brushed the woman's shoulder-length auburn hair back from the collar of a creamy mocha blouse. Bright blue eyes, a sign of happiness, lifted to meet hers. "Hi," she murmured.

Brenna rested her hands on Cassidy's shoulders and they both for a moment existed only in each other's gaze. It was a dazzling feeling for Cassidy and she leaned close to kiss Brenna. A chair leg scraped against the floor. Cassidy felt Brenna brush her shoulder and the lingering kiss she'd hoped for became a quick peck to the corner of her lips. Then she squeezed Cassidy's hand as she passed behind her. "Thank you for holding dinner."

Cassidy turned to follow and the women settled into seats at the table side by side.

"Chicken looks lovely."

"Mommy made it for us," Ryan stated. "It's good."

"You haven't eaten it yet," Cassidy reminded her son.

"But you always makes a good dinner," Ryan stated.

"That's true." Brenna leaned toward Ryan and cupped his hand holding his fork. Underneath the table, she also caressed Cassidy's thigh. "Your mother is an excellent cook." She let go of Ryan's hand and Cassidy's thigh and took her napkin into her lap, looking across the table where James and Thomas sat. "I'd like to hear all about your day," she said. "But first, let's say grace."

"I'm giving this one to Thomas since it was his last day at school," James said.

Thomas picked up Ryan's right hand and Brenna took the little boy's left. Everyone else linked around the table. "Dear Lord, we thank you for the blessings of nature with this food. Amen."

"Amen," echoed around the table and then Thomas, who had the chicken platter next to him, served himself a sizable breast while giving Ryan a chicken leg. Both Cassidy and Brenna dug into their salads first.

"So how did your meeting go?" Cassidy asked quietly.

"My copies of the script and contract are being sent over by courier next week." Brenna looked up from her dish and asked, "Thomas, what's your graduation schedule?"

"I have all that in my bag," he replied. "Next week's full of mandatory meetings and the graduation is Sunday afternoon at the campus auditorium."

"If I remember correctly, we need tickets. You have a limited number."

"I got four."

"Have you heard back from your father?" Brenna asked. Cassidy heard the quaver in her lover's voice. Brenna's first husband who was the father of her two boys, lived in northern California. Cassidy had only met Brenna's second husband, now also an ex, a few times.

"He sent a card with a check. Says he can't make it. He has a show opening next weekend."

When Brenna rolled her bottom lip between her teeth, Cassidy knew she was swallowing down her words, likely because they would be as stormy as her now-gray eyes. "All right. Who would you like to be there?"

"There's four of us here," Thomas said. His calm tone suggested he had already thought about this. His words to her confirmed it. "Cass, would you and Ryan want to attend my graduation?"

"Those can be long. Are you sure?" She looked significantly toward Ryan who was stabbing peas on his plate. He was generally a well-behaved child, but a long graduation ceremony was not going to interest him except for the moments Thomas was involved. Her son had adored Thomas ever since they first met at a warehouse outdoors supply store the previous fall. Maybe, she thought, if Ryan is told this was something special for Thomas, he might make it through most of the event without an issue.

"Yeah. Hey, bud," Thomas drew Ryan's attention away from his food for a moment. "I'm going to go to a big ceremony with my friends next weekend. You wanna come?"

"A seer-mony? What for?"

"I'm finished with school, so we're celebrating."

"I don't even start school," Ryan said. Cassidy bit her lip as she watched and listened to her son processing the invitation.

Thomas was smiling indulgently. "I know, but you will."

"When I go to school with you?"

"Not exactly. This wouldn't be school for you, not yet. Just a party about school."

"I don't have to study?" Cassidy smiled. He'd obviously watched Thomas and James many times over the last few months reading their textbooks and completing assignments.

"Nope."

"Okay, then I go." Ryan held up his greasy fingers from eating his chicken leg by hand and made an 'O' with his first finger and thumb.

"Okay." Brenna brushed Ryan's hair from his face and kissed his temple. "So it will be the four of us there."

Cassidy reached under the table and took Brenna's hand in her own. They'd only been out all together a few times, mostly to shops or area parks. This was unmistakably a public family event. She hoped all of them attending was the right thing to do. "All right," she agreed.

James asked, "Is this a suit and tie thing?"

Brenna shook her head. "We'll all dress up a bit for pictures. But I don't see a reason to subject you to a tie, darling."

James laughed and flopped back in his chair. "Thank god."

Ryan echoed James. "Thank god!" and made everyone laugh.

Once everyone had cleared their own dishes to the kitchen, Brenna excused the boys to their rooms. "We'll watch some TV in a bit, but right now I could use a little quiet." She took the remaining platters and silverware to the counter and started finding containers for the few leftovers.

Cassidy entered after her, taking down a bottle from the wine rack. "Want a glass?"

"I'm good," Brenna said as she found spaces in the refrigerator for two small square containers.

"You have a high school graduate." Cassidy leaned back against the counter as she examined the foil around the bottle's neck. "That's something to celebrate."

"Not yet. Next week," Brenna said. She took the wine from Cassidy and leaned forward to put it up and away. Her height meant she pressed tightly against Cassidy in the process. The blonde's hands went to her hips. "I got it."

"And I've got you," Cassidy murmured in her ear before pressing a kiss against the curve.

Brenna groaned and then bit her lip, arousal stoked. Cassidy, however, was far from finished.

Her hands slipped around Brenna's back, molding their fronts tightly together. The blonde was warm and soft. Brenna's hands grasped Cassidy's shoulders as full lips slid from her ear to the junction of her shoulder and neck. "Oh, god," she breathed.

Cassidy chuckled. "So, are you going to tell me what's bothering you?" She breathed over Brenna's lips, "Or am I going to have to kiss you a bit more?"

"I'm sorry I was late for dinner."

"I already told you it's all right. Meetings with agents can be unpredictable things."

"But you're here, cooking, and watching the bo–"

Cassidy put a hand on Brenna's shoulder. "They only arrived home a few minutes ahead of you."

That diverted Brenna. "Why were they late?"

"Thomas drove James by Isis to work on one of his projects."

"Oh." Brenna sighed. "I know we agreed I'd take the movie in Ireland, but you'll be coming back here and be their only adult for weeks."

"We'll just work from my house for a while. And James and Thomas can stay mostly on their own here, you know that."

Brenna exhaled and wrapped her arms around Cassidy's waist. The blonde's arms slid tightly around her back in reply. "I want to be a better partner."

"So, do the dishes and then come sit with me on the couch for a family movie," Cassidy replied easily. "I'll check on the boys."

Brenna didn't immediately release Cassidy after she spoke. Instead she lifted one hand to the blonde's cheek, caressing the delicate jaw with her thumb. Sliding her hand around the back of Cassidy's neck, playing with the fine hairs at the nape, she pressed her lips in a tender kiss. "I love you."

"I love you, too," Cassidy murmured, immediately starting to nuzzle Brenna's throat again.

"All right, all right. Go." Brenna chuckled and pushed her away reluctantly. "I'll be done quickly."

Full lips turned up in a broad smile. "Good."

Brenna turned to the sink and started running the water, watching Cassidy walk to the bedroom hallway to see what their sons were doing.

Ryan wanted to watch a movie, but the time was late and even though a movie had been the idea, Cassidy didn't want her son up past his bedtime. It would be a fight if they all remained up and active after the youngest was put to sleep, so they all agreed instead to play dominoes. While the game was simple enough for Ryan to play, it held James and Thomas's attentions. A large double-nine set was retrieved from the back of one of Brenna's closets. Five tiles instead of seven dealt to each of them and the group was off and playing. Brenna and Cassidy sat on the couch, Ryan kneeling and taking his turn between theirs. Thomas and James sat on floor cushions on the other side of the coffee table.

Cassidy watched as Ryan placed a tile with a two-dot end against another two-dot tile, leaving his five-dot end open. Brenna looked around the board then sighed. "There's no more tiles to draw but I don't have a tile to play," she said. "Pass."

"You can have mine," Ryan said. He picked one up from his two remaining and held it toward her.

The other woman looked at the tile and gave it a look of serious consideration. After a moment though, she shook her head, cupped his chin, then kissed Ryan's cheek, brushing lightly with her thumb at the faint rose imprint left by her lipstick. "Thank you, Ryan, but I can't place it. It's your tile. Rules are I have to pass. You wait for your next turn and place it yourself." She looked up at James. "James, your turn."

James found a spot for one of his two remaining tiles and play passed to Thomas. Cassidy realized she would be able to go out with her turn no matter where Thomas placed one of his last two tiles. Thomas played his tile, a three-dot with a blank on the other end.

Cassidy placed her last tile on an open end of track near James. "I'm out. I win."

"I hafta lay my tile, Mommy."

"Game's over. I'm the first one with no tiles."

"Bu-" He started to his feet.

"No," she interrupted, putting a hand on his over his tiles. "It's time for bed anyway."

Ryan's bottom lip jutted out and his eyes drew close and narrowed. She realized he was angry, but she was so surprised to see the expression she wasn't prepared for his next action. He burst up and shoved at the entire layout on the table. "No!" The tiles went off the other side into Thomas's lap and the floor.

"Hey!" James objected, picking up a tile.

Picking tiles from his own lap, Thomas said quietly, "Ryan, we can play again another time."

Cassidy's face filled with heat, embarrassed by her son's outburst. She stood and picked him up.

Ryan squirmed hard in her arms and she saw him open his mouth.

"Do not scream," she admonished firmly. "They have agreed to play another time. You need to apologize for making a mess. Then we'll go home."

Brenna stood. "But-"

A quick look from Cassidy cut off Brenna. Then she refocused on her son. "Well," she prompted, "What do you say?" Her son had stopped squirming and looked to be transitioning from anger to tears. She realized he was too tired to be rational. Hugging him close, she said gently, "Just say you are sorry."

Ryan looked at her, tears leaking down his cheeks, and said, "I'm sorry, Mommy."

"And James and Thomas." She nodded toward the boys who were getting to their feet.

"I sorry them too."

"And Brenna?"

"She said I could put my tile." His tone was accusing.

"She couldn't know I would go out. When the game is over, it's over, Ryan. No one else plays any tiles. Those are the rules."

Cassidy felt Brenna's hand brush Ryan's back above her own arm. "It's hard to lose, but we enjoyed playing, didn't we?" Brenna said, looking from Ryan to her sons.

"Yep," said James. Thomas nodded.

"See? You don't have to win to have fun," Cassidy said.

"Can we play again now?"

"No, it's late. We will play again another time."

"There's no reason for you to drive home. We can all fit here," Brenna said.

"You're sure?" Cassidy asked.

"Of course I'm sure."

"All right."

"Let's go set up the bed in the spare room."

"I have some things to do before school tomorrow," James said. "I'll be in my room."

Brenna stopped him. Cassidy knew by the silent tilt of her lover's head and the nod from James, that she was checking her son was all right following Ryan's emotional outburst. Brenna's younger son, though a teenager, was a sensitive soul. Thomas, already eighteen, had been his usual problem-solving self.

Cassidy noticed James took his cell phone, which had sat by his knee throughout the game, with him. A teen's social existence, it seemed, was tethered to their phone. Back in high school she had spent hours on her parents' second phone line talking to her friends long into the night too. James at least had the ability to talk in the privacy of his room.

"Lights out by ten," Brenna reminded him.

"I know." James stepped forward and Brenna kissed his cheek. "Good night."

Thomas was just closing the top of the storage case for the dominoes. Cassidy asked, "Did you find them all?"

"Yeah, no problem." He rubbed Ryan's shoulder. "Good night, bud, see you in the morning."

Ryan rubbed his eyes; Thomas smiled at Cassidy and stepped back.

"What's your schedule tomorrow?" Brenna touched her elder son's shoulder as he started to pass her.

He shrugged. "Sleeping in. Some of us are picnicking for lunch at Rustic Canyon Park."

"Just let me know if you won't be home in time for dinner."

He kissed her cheek. "Will do. Good night, Mom."

"Good night."

Carrying Ryan, Cassidy followed Brenna to the spare room. Halfway through the process when Brenna pulled out a set of pajamas for Ryan from a closet shelf, she was struck how common them staying the night had become. She realized she and Brenna were rapidly passing through several relationship stages and they hadn't talked extensively about it. They'd agreed to a "family" vacation before Brenna's movie shoot—huge considering they would be going to an entirely different country.

They discussed projects they were offered or wanted to do, but decisions largely didn't affect them as a couple as long as the projects were in L.A. Still, the fact remained they were two single mothers running separate households. Cassidy couldn't recall the last time she'd slept alone in her own house.

She had a sudden revelation. Unlike her previous relationships this one wasn't headed toward marriage. Despite how bad her marriage to Mitch had become by the end, the word still said 'security' to her.

"Brenna," she asked as they stepped out to the hallway, closing the spare room's door behind them, "What do you think of marriage?"

"I'm rather shit at it actually," Brenna said. She hesitantly turned and blue-gray eyes found her. "Why?"

"Would you want to get married at some point?"

"We can't."

"I know. Legally. But, what if? I don't know... like a commitment, or more papers like the directives we signed in the hospital?" Brenna paused in the hallway. After a moment being studied where she was unable to decipher all the different emotions on Brenna's face, Cassidy asked, "Do you think we could talk about it?"

"Right now? I thought you had something else on your mind for our private time?"

Cassidy frowned. Her time with Brenna without Ryan underfoot was limited. "I think we could do both," she said. "I'd like to know."

"All right," Brenna said. She opened the door to her bedroom, letting Cassidy enter first, then shut it behind them. Cassidy heard the click of the lock so they couldn't be accidentally disturbed.

The master bedroom had an ensuite bathroom and Brenna headed for it. "Why don't you change in here? You still have a robe on the door."

It was a reminder, again, how often Cassidy had been over for the night. "Do you remember the first time I slept over?" she asked. Brenna nodded. "What went through your mind?"

"I was just so glad you were safe," she said and Cassidy heard a slight exhale of relief. Then Brenna added, "I also enjoyed the next morning. Very much."

As she removed her clothes behind the bathroom door, Cassidy remembered their shared shower, Brenna gifting her with a sweatshirt, and the sweet, sweet sex they had before emerging to the noises of their sons interacting. Stepping out of the bathroom while tying the robe around her nakedness, Cassidy asked, "Did you think 'I'd like to do this every day'?"

Instead of answering immediately, Brenna, who had exchanged her clothes for a nightgown, stepped forward and wrapped her arms around Cassidy's waist. Kissing her on the side of her neck, she asked, "Did you?"

"I think I did," Cassidy said, stepping out of Brenna's embrace, but keeping hold of her hand as she sat down on the edge of the bed. "Over the next few months every time we were apart I was thinking of when we could be together again."

"So was I," Brenna said. She eased onto the bed next to Cassidy, still clasping her hand. "And when you were here, after the hospital, yes, I did think this would be wonderful if it could be all the time. I'd been really scared I might have lost you before..." Brenna voice trailed off even as her hands slipped up Cassidy's wrists to her elbows. Her eyes were glassy when they met Cassidy's.

"Yeah," Cassidy said. The emotion they shared gave her a lump in her throat. "I *love* you," she said, feeling the emotion intensely. "I want this forever," she said after a moment to take a breath.

"What do you want to do?" Brenna asked.

"As you said, we can't get married, not legally, but...I-I want what a ceremony means: me swearing to be always here for you, you always here for me, us raising our sons, figuring out what's good for all of us together. I wan-" Brenna laid her fingers against Cassidy's lips, stopping the flow.

She nodded. "Okay, yes, I want those too. Fidelity, faithfulness, promises to love, honor, cherish-til death us do part." She shook her head then. "But I've failed so miserably at that. Twice."

"Is it just the word holding you up?"

"Lapsed Catholic," Brenna said wryly. "I think it's ingrained."

Cassidy nodded. "It has the weight of security for me. But-"

"You suggested a commitment," Brenna interrupted and her hesitating tone suggested she was thinking through several things. "Maybe there's some ceremony we can find or create ourselves," Brenna said. "To say what *we* want it to say about this. Us. Our relationship, making you feel secure, matters to me. Yes, like you, I feel I'm yours and you're... well... mine." Brenna's face turned red and she dropped her eyes. "That sounds so damn possessive," she muttered then lifted her head and continued. "But I don't want to control you. Like you, I see it as another step in us being together. Raising Ryan. I know Thomas is almost grown and James would likely inform us he doesn't need parenting anymore but, yes, I see you as their other parent. We're *partners* as I said at the cast party. In *everything*."

Cassidy was stunned silent at Brenna's notion of commitment. She hadn't thought that succinctly about it, but apparently Brenna had. "We should do something."

"Maybe we could talk to some other long-term couples. Find out what they've done."

"Weren't the women who owned the Isis gallery partners?" Cassidy asked. "The art teacher?"

Brenna tilted her head to the right, a sign she was thinking back through memories. "I believe so."

"I think we have a plan then," Cassidy said. She leaned forward and softly pressed her lips to Brenna's. When they parted, Brenna lifted her eyes, and Cassidy saw they had become soft blue. "Time to sleep?"

"Time to go to bed," Cassidy corrected. All this talk of commitment had her feeling like they were embarking on a new path. Together. She reached out and tugged at the neckline of Brenna's nightgown, causing the fabric to fall off one shoulder, giving her a full view of smooth collarbone. "If we're going act married, I definitely want a wedding night." Her thumb drifted over the skin, drawing down the fabric further.

Brenna's cheeks flushed again making Cassidy chuckle. Drawing the other woman's chin up she brought their lips together in another sweet, slow kiss. In her head she fancied hearing, *You may now kiss the bride,* and it made her smile widen against Brenna's lips. Bren might be the lapsed Catholic, but Cassidy hadn't realized how much she had internalized about marriage as a required step in cementing a relationship.

Deepening the kiss, Cassidy wondered if a real marriage might ever be possible. For right now though, she was determined to make Brenna know in the deepest parts of her soul that Cassidy was thoroughly needy to possess her, body and soul. Repeatedly.

She stroked down both Brenna's arms and eased the woman back until the nightgown was a puddle of silk on the sheets and she held the other woman's naked hips in her hands. Brenna's fingers settled over hers. She took them in a light grip and spread their arms wide. For a long silent moment she simply drank in the sight of the woman's freckled skin and soft curves.

Moving her legs full length over the sheets, Cassidy drew Brenna on her knees forward between her thighs. She tucked her ankles over the backs of Brenna's calves, trapping her lover. Tenderly she guided Brenna's hands to her shoulders, then slid her own down Brenna's arms, around her ribs, and behind the other woman's back. Their bodies intimately entwined, she luxuriously nibbled at Brenna's lips until they parted and she continued to lushly lick the soft inner flesh of the woman's mouth.

Feeling Brenna's heart quicken against her chest, Cassidy finally dipped her head to Brenna's modest breasts. She inhaled the warm scent of vanilla, coffee, and jasmine before circling her tongue around a taut nipple. Brenna slid her hands into Cassidy's hair and arched her body upward. Biting the nipple in her teeth, Cassidy relished Brenna's groan. "Oh, god. Cass. Mm."

Brenna sagged. Cassidy's grip held her up and she continued to taste and tease, enjoying her lover's voice humming and gasping and starting syllables of probably a dozen different words only to be unable to complete them. Nipping pliant skin, licking, then biting Brenna's rapidly hardening nipples, Cassidy sought every point of arousal she had learned over their few months together.

When Brenna's hips began to rock, Cassidy rearranged them so she was atop Brenna and shifted her knee to increase the pressure on her lover's center. Keeping one arm behind her lover's head, Cassidy slipped her other hand down quivering stomach muscles until she sifted her fingertips through the short strands covering her mound. Heat and moisture met her exploration and Brenna hummed her approval when Cassidy brushed a fingertip against her swelling clit.

Rubbing Brenna's clit, Cassidy fingers grew increasingly wetter. She sucked at hardening nipples until Brenna body was arching up into her mouth, needy.

Brenna kissed her, pushing Cassidy back instead, and sat up, nuzzling into Cassidy's breasts.

Then Cassidy rolled them both over again and returned her fingers to Brenna's center, this time as they lay side by side. Up on one bent arm Cassidy studied Brenna's body while she stroked her folds. Brenna's skin had a flush all the way down her chest and her eyes had become an even darker blue.

"Cass," Brenna breathed and her hips rose to meet Cassidy's strokes.

"You are so beautiful," she murmured, lowering her head and kissing at the corner of Brenna's jaw where it met her ear. "I love how your body responds to my touch."

Brenna's hands cupped Cassidy's face and her fingers slid over Cassidy's cheeks. Closing her eyes when Brenna kissed her, Cassidy felt her way deeper into Brenna's body, two fingers ressing and turning and pushing her lover closer and closer to fulfillment. Each gasp, each hitched breath, and each sound Brenna made created a song Cassidy was sure she would never tire of hearing. "God, Cass, I–"

Intimate muscles tightly squeezed Cassidy's fingers and Brenna lifted her hips, grasping Cassidy's hand to hold it in place.

"Mm mm!" When Brenna shut her eyes tightly, arching her neck, her inner channel tightened further around Cassidy's fingers. She moved them to keep the other woman on edge before curling them up and catching just the right spot. "Oh!" Cassidy finally felt her fingers being released. Brenna's hard breaths into Cassidy's shoulder kept the noise to a minimum as Cassidy coaxed several more shuddering peaks from Brenna's body. Eventually Brenna exhaled.

Cassidy, however, wasn't done just yet. Sliding to the floor on her knees, she grasped Brenna's hips and dragged her toward the edge of the bed. Tucking Brenna's legs over her shoulders, Cassidy lapped up the post-orgasmic cream from her center. Fingers gripped her hair and Cassidy relished each aftershock fluttering against her lips and tongue. "Mm," she hummed her own pleasure, the vibrations making Brenna shudder again.

"Oh, damn, g..."

Gradually and reluctantly, Cassidy pulled away from throbbing, tasty flesh. Standing between Brenna's knees and held in place by the deep blue eyes watching her every motion, Cassidy lifted her fingers to the collar of her robe, pushing it from her shoulders until it puddled on the floor. Love and appreciation called her silently forward and she crawled backed onto the bed. Tenderly she gathered the other woman in her arms, nuzzled auburn hair and entwined their legs. Finally, Cassidy buried her face in Brenna's neck, relishing the security found in her arms.

"Thomas Lanigan."

Standing at the podium in the auditorium, the school's principal boomed out her son's name.

Brenna rose with Ryan in her arms, Cassidy holding her left shoulder. On her right, James cupped his hands around his mouth and hooted. Brenna pointed at the stage, talking to Ryan, "There he is." Ryan waved. Brenna didn't think Thomas could see them clearly in the crowded space, but she felt her heart beat faster when the flash from Cassidy's camera went off beside her. "He looks good," she said as a way to calm herself.

Ryan waved again. James hollered, "Yeah, man! Go, bro!"

"At least he's no longer nervous," Cassidy replied, leaning close to Brenna's ear. "I really thought he was going to sweat his way through his second shirt."

That morning Thomas had sat down with Cassidy where he thought he was out of earshot of Brenna, his mother, and confessed his anxiety about the day and his future. "What you said to him helped," Brenna said. "Thank you."

Cassidy lifted her arm around Brenna's back and kissed Ryan's temple then hers. "That's what family does."

Brenna felt the conviction in her lover's voice and nodded in agreement. Cassidy's hand moved from her back to her far shoulder, soothing Brenna's tension. She looked around, seeing other parents, husbands and wives, tucked together in the same sort of intimacy as their children walked across the stage to receive their diplomas. She looked across her shoulder to James, caught his eye and smiled at him, earning a smile in return.

"We are family," she agreed, leaning her head against Cassidy's.

FAMILY FUNCTIONS

Altadena, California
June 2001

CASSIDY COULD see a slight strain pinching Brenna's brow as she made the final turn onto Alaca Drive. It was late afternoon and the woman had been driving all day from the north California mountains. Brenna's right hand rested on the center console, and Cassidy moved her left over it, squeezing the fine boned fingers lightly. In response, the corner of Brenna's lips curved.

The sun had been good for her lover, Cassidy thought, caressing Brenna's patrician features with her gaze. Brenna's tan had deepened to a soft gold, complimenting her auburn locks and making her blue eyes more vivid. Cassidy looked down at their entwined hands and noticed she, too, had gotten a significant tan, but her skin remained considerably lighter than Brenna's. She also imagined her expression was just as relaxed. Being out in nature always rejuvenated her, something they both had in common.

The Mountaineer jerked suddenly and stopped, making Cassidy grasp for the dashboard. Her attention shot from their hands to the street ahead.

Several kids ran over makeshift ramps with dirt bikes, skateboards and inline skates. Seeing a blond child picking himself and a bike off the pavement just a dozen feet ahead of Brenna's bumper, Cassidy realized Brenna had hit the brakes when he fell toward the street. She winced in empathy as another child with honey brown hair, and probably eight or nine years old, tumbled off of a ramp on the sidewalk when the skate wheel caught on a corner. Despite wearing a helmet she took several seconds to get up. When she did, she looked in dismay at the scrapes on her arms and legs. However, both children were soon again running full tilt at the ramp, encouraged by cheers from several companions.

"Nice neighborhood." The comment drew Cassidy's head around to look back over her shoulder. Brenna's older teen son, Thomas, leaned on the window, looking around. He brushed dark hair from in front of his eyes as he met her gaze briefly. Next to him, Brenna's other teen son, James, rubbed his elbow, obviously having struck it on the door in their sudden stop. Each boy had a steadying arm across the sleeping body of Cassidy's five-year-old son, Ryan, laying across their laps.

Brenna spoke up. "You are not getting a skateboard."

Cassidy watched Thomas shrug but smile. "I have keys to the car. What do I need with a skateboard?"

"I'm just going on record," Brenna replied.

Cassidy laughed and moved her left hand between Brenna's neck and the headrest, brushing her fingers through the ends of auburn curls. She looked forward through the windshield at the street activity – noting all children had scattered to the sidewalks — and Brenna drove forward once more.

When the Mountaineer pulled to a stop in her own home's driveway, Cassidy could see into the rear yard of her neighbor's home. Obviously hearing the engine, Mrs. Sandsmarsh, wearing her customary house dress, turned away from hanging laundry in her backyard. The older woman raised her arm in greeting, and she waved in reply.

Stepping out onto the grass, Cassidy closed the passenger door and critically inspected the front lawn and entrance to her home. She did like living with Brenna, but she was unsure about making the arrangement official. It was, she knew, a point of contention between them, but she was fond of her little house, the first acquired on her own. Out front, the hedges breaking up the hard line of privacy fence looked more square than she remembered. Fresh plantings, evidenced by newly turned dirt and mulch, had been put in the gardens to either side of her entry stoop.

Looking over at Brenna, she inclined her head toward the garden work. "Your doing?"

Her lover smiled sheepishly. "Not all of it. I sent your address to my regular service and asked them to fix up anything else that needed it."

"You knew I'd want to come here eventually." Cassidy walked around the front of the SUV to meet Brenna shifting her weight diffidently on the stone step. Cassidy watched Brenna swallow as she tilted her head back to meet Cassidy's gaze. "Thank you."

Lifting the other woman's chin, Cassidy pressed her lips to Brenna's. Then she wrapped her arms around her lover and deepened the kiss.

When Cassidy let her take a step back, Brenna asked, "Who says I wasn't doing it to improve the curbside value so you could sell?"

Gauging the remark and Brenna's expressive features with a raised eyebrow, Cassidy finally shook her head. "I know that isn't why you did it."

Brenna exhaled. "You're right. It isn't. Did you want to go inside before we fetch the dog?"

"I can put him in a kennel. I should," Cassidy insisted. "I know you agreed we could take him on vacation with us, but that's when we thought Mike Cutter's cabin was available. That was private space. But the public campground would've been too much."

Brenna's gaze turned troubled. "Ryan misses him."

"Yes, but Ranger's trained as a guard dog. He knows Ryan, yes, and even now Thomas and James have been around a few times. But some kid in the public area of the campground comes running up to him, and that's a big liability."

Brenna let out a sigh. "Yes, I know. I still want to fix this."

"We had a great time camping. Ryan didn't mention him once." Cassidy had decided to leave Ranger with the Talbots when they'd changed their plans.

"He was too busy playing tag or learning to belly flop from Thomas."

Cassidy laughed. "And cannonballs from James."

Brenna started to fish in her purse. "Looking for the key?" When she nodded, Cassidy withdrew her own keys from her handbag. "I've got it."

Stepping up to her doorway, she heard Brenna call out behind her. "Boys!"

All three of their sons looked up where they were playing tag in the yard. Her five-year-old son, Ryan, was "it." Brenna's sons, Thomas, seventeen, and James, just recently turned sixteen, were keeping only a short distance away from him. Apparently the unspoken rule was not to truly outrun Ryan. She was inordinately pleased how thoroughly now James and Thomas played the role of older brothers to her son. It had made living together under one roof manageable. They still hadn't discussed long term plans though Brenna had joked about Cassidy selling her home.

Ryan finally reached her side. "Whatcha doing, Mommy?"

"Would you like to show Thomas and James your room?"

"Really?" Her son's face brightened when she nodded, and he ran back out to Thomas and James who were coming closer at a more leisurely walk.

"You see my room?" he asked them. James shrugged, but Thomas nodded, and Ryan grabbed his hand. Cassidy and Brenna stepped back as Ryan dragged Thomas past them into the home. If he was upset by Ryan's handling of him, Thomas didn't show it. Shrugging again and stuffing his hands now stuffed in his pockets, James followed them.

Withdrawing her key from the deadbolt and replacing it in her purse, Cassidy felt a hand on her shoulder. She turned her head to see Brenna's gaze following their children. The compact woman's eyes had turned gray, something she had often seen when Brenna admitted to being emotionally upset. Ryan was undeniably enthusiastic.

With her free hand, she grasped Brenna's hand with a gentle squeeze. "Come on in."

Brenna entered first, walking past her through the open doorway, and looked around the dark interior. Cassidy turned and closed her front door then flipped on the entry light before making a slow walking survey of her house. Brenna trailed a step behind. A bleach smell overlaid with lemon greeted Cassidy when she entered her kitchen. She noticed several little things, like the under-sink wastebasket was empty, and the refrigerator had been washed free of dirty fingerprints. The sliding glass leading to the screened porch had also been wiped spotless.

"Thank you," Cassidy said.

Using her body, she crowded Brenna up against the separating wall between the living room and the kitchen. Small and delicate, but strong, hands wrapped around her upper arms, and then deft fingers sifted into her hair. Watching gray eyes warm to blue, Cassidy kissed Brenna, lingering to absorb the feelings of relief, happiness, and sensual pleasure that came from being able to do this with someone who so clearly demonstrated her love.

"It means a lot to me that you thought to look into things." She gently cupped Brenna's cheek.

"Did you want anything to take back... to the other house?" It was obvious Brenna had paused in order to change her word choice.

She'd already gotten Brenna to bring her checkbook. She needed to collect her newest bills, and maybe the actual files where she kept her receipts. A handful of movies and demo tapes on loan from her agent were tidily stacked on the shelves next to the television and multimedia player. She probably should get those back to the agency. She had several Disney characters and ceramic Hummel original figurines, but knick-knacks should probably be left behind for now. However one pair of figures drew her attention and made her cross the room to open the display cabinet.

Brenna followed Cassidy into her living room out of curiosity. Looking over Cassidy's shoulder, she identified the figurines the blonde lifted out and raised her brow. "Rocky and Bullwinkle?" she said.

"Your very first gift to me," Cassidy reminded her, tracing the buck-toothed smile of Rocky the Flying Squirrel who posed with outstretched arms.

"Well, second." Brenna took the Bullwinkle statuette gingerly and shook her head. Cassidy noticed her lip curled and looked at the moose's bewildered expression. Brenna traced the comb-like antlers with a finger. "Remember the slippers back in October?"

Cassidy's smile warmed immediately. "Oh my aching feet," she laughed. "Yeah."

"I'd planned to give those to you for your birthday," Brenna admitted. "But you looked so miserable."

"I should collect those too, while I'm here." Cassidy turned to the bedroom hallway. "Come on. I've got the box for these still in my closet."

She led Brenna to her bedroom, passing the doorway to Ryan's on the way. Looking inside the child's room, Brenna watched Thomas sitting patiently as Ryan filled his lap with a variety of toys. Among them was Harry, the handmade monster from "Where the Wild Things Are" that Brenna had gifted to him for his fifth birthday.

"Do you have any other empty boxes?" she asked Cassidy, after finally following her into the bedroom to see she had already stepped into her walk-in closet.

"Yes, why?" Cassidy asked as she moved several things to get at something on the back of a high shelf.

"Ryan's claiming half his bedroom for taking back to the house."

Finally, their business done at Cassidy's home, Brenna shut the rear of the Mountaineer with the boxes inside, which included several of the dog's things. With neither of them working at the moment, the house would be quiet and Brenna had convinced Cassidy that she could take Ranger instead of putting him up in yet another kennel.

Cassidy adjusted her position in the passenger seat, admittedly stiff, sore, and extremely tired. She had to be careful. Her injuries of only a few months earlier would cause lingering discomfort for years to come. She had thought they could walk over to the Talbot home since it was only on the next corner. Now belting herself into the seat, she was grateful Brenna had insisted they had to load the dog into the back of the SUV anyway.

With Brenna's permission, however, Thomas walked Ryan to the Talbot's house, James trailing behind. The trio stopped a few times to talk with other children gathered and playing in the streets.

Brenna parked along the curb. Cassidy saw Lou Talbot under the hood of the family's Buick. Two children played in the yard. Ranger bounded enthusiastically between them as they tossed a tennis ball back and forth. She recognized the Talbot's two children. Chance, Ryan's age, had gotten thinner and taller, and Deter a couple years older.

Ranger was a Dalmatian with a lean body typical of the breed. However Cassidy thought she noticed a tightness around his ribs suggesting he had become too thin. She stepped down from the front passenger seat to the grassy curb.

Ryan was already running up, having spotted both his dog and his best friend. "Chance!"

No doubt hearing the clattering of doors, dogs, and children, Lou Talbot backed up from his car.

When his gaze found her, she said, "Hello, Lou." Slowly she walked up the driveway.

"Hold up," he said quickly. "I told Gwen to pack the things. We'll bring them out and you can be on your way."

"Gwen's inside? I'll go in and see her," Cassidy said, ignoring his tone, though she heard a note of anxiety in it.

Lou stepped further away from his car, clearly wanting to impede her. Though also for some reason, he seemed wary of getting too close. So, though she would rather have not, Cassidy did stop. She studied him with interest, noting the short-sleeve shirt he wore might have been office attire at one time. Now, however, it was covered in irreparable oil and sweat stains.

His gaze narrowed at the same time she sensed Brenna stepping up to her left side.

"Good afternoon," Brenna offered with a smile.

Lou started to clean his hands on his shirt, looking rattled. He snapped up a rag from the chassis and rubbed his hands with it.

"Good to see you again," Brenna added. Her smile never faltered.

"Uh. Yeah." His brow creased. "Have we met?"

"Not formally." Brenna held out her hand. Her tone dropped a register, deepening to a husky silk when she gave her name. "Brenna Lanigan."

Lou was about to automatically take the hand when, suddenly, his brows tightened, his smile froze, and he immediately pulled back his hand. At the curl of his lip, Cassidy imagined the word "lesbians" in bloody red dripping script scrolling behind his narrowing eyes. "Wait here." His tone was curt and he turned his back on both of them, striding up the short walk to his front stoop before he disappeared inside the brick home.

"That went well," Brenna commented wryly, dropping her hand to her side. Cassidy grasped her hand, also unsettled by the reaction.

"Mom, how can you say that? He was insulted just by your presence."

Cassidy and Brenna turned to see James just straightening up next to one of the Talbot children. He walked over to them, a deep frown darkening his features. "You should have told him off."

"We're only here for the dog," Brenna pointed out. "It's not useful to get upset." Cassidy looked toward the home's door and Brenna put a hand on her shoulder.

"I'd hoped to see Gwen though," Cassidy admitted when she felt Brenna's touch.

The front door opened again; Cassidy straightened. Brenna

dropped her hand to the small of Cassidy's back, unseen but still supporting.

Lou stepped out carrying a large plastic bag; Gwen stood behind him partially in the shadows. Cassidy reflexively smiled at her friend. Gwen gave a quick look to her husband's back then nodded briefly in acknowledgment. The expression on her face was distressingly unreadable.

"Here." Lou passed Cassidy the large bag, so far away from them that his right arm was fully extended just to reach her. She stretched out her arm and took the neck of the bag below his hand. "Now get out of here before someone sees you."

He turned back to his car. Stunned by his blunt dismissal, Cassidy and Brenna both jumped when he exploded suddenly.

"What the fuck are you doing?! Get the hell away from there!"

Everyone's gaze focused on the scene as Lou ran at his car waving his arms and continuing to yell. Standing near the open car hood, Ranger lifted his head and licked his muzzle. Cassidy watched the dog's shoulders drop, his hind legs extend and his ears drop back.

The Dalmatian had been trained as a guard dog. He bared his teeth. She heard the single warning bark and then the growl.

No one reached Lou before Ranger did.

Brenna did not know what to do first. When Ranger leaped on Lou Talbot, she saw Ryan on the ground behind them, crawling out from underneath the car.

She did not want him to go for the dog or, considering its current behavior, for the dog to switch its attention to Ryan. She started around the back of the car to coax Ryan to come to her, keeping the car between him and the wrestling animal and man.

However, Cassidy's voice froze her in place after only a single step.

"Ranger! Down!"

Everyone froze in place and stared at Cassidy. Her attention went to the Dalmatian. "Ranger," she called, voice firm. "Back."

The dog pawed at Lou's chest, looked down at the man then over to Ryan and back up to Cassidy. Maintaining eye contact, Cassidy took a step forward. "Back," she called again. "Down."

Swaying side to side, Ranger barked at her.

"Cass!"

Not looking at Brenna, Cassidy responded, "I'm serious, Bren.

Don't move."

Ryan stood with a wet tennis ball in his hands. He looked at Ranger standing over Lou. The big man was covering his face. "Ranger, let's play."

Brenna bit her lip. The dog turned toward the young boy's voice. *Was he recognizing a family face?*

Lou burst upright with both hands in that moment, taking the dog off its feet with a shove. "God damned mutt!"

A melee ensued. Ranger growled, all teeth and claws, and Lou yelled, fists flying. Cassidy, to Brenna's dismay, waded in. "Cass!"

Between the barking dog and rolling bodies, Cassidy grabbed hold of the Dalmatian's collar. Then with a yell that was clearly agony, Cassidy was also pulled down by the leaping dog.

Now Brenna didn't hesitate. She swept forward, shoved Ryan toward Thomas, and yelled for someone to call 911. Closing her eyes, she dove for the Dalmatian, wrapping her arms around its stomach. Ranger yelped. Brenna held him and curled up in a ball, protecting her head and face by pushing them into the dog's back. The dog's claws scratched at the air.

"Damn!" Cassidy's voice dropped out, then she yelled again. "Ranger, come!"

Brenna let go. Her senses told her the dog had backed off. Opening one eye, Brenna watched Ranger lick his muzzle in her direction and then lope to Cassidy's side. Cassidy took hold of his collar when he came within arm's reach. "Sit." The Dalmatian sat, tail flat on the ground behind him and ears down.

"What the hell was that all about?" Lou demanded. The dog's ears straightened up at the sound.

Cassidy said, "I was certain I told Gwen you never, ever charge at Ranger."

"He was in the car!"

Ranger's head swung toward Lou again. Cassidy looked at the car. Ryan still stood by the open hood. "Ranger, ball!" He waved it at the dog. "Come play!"

Brenna finally uncurled and gestured for him to come to her. In Ryan's hands, Cassidy noticed the tennis ball was wet. "Where did you get that, Ryan?" she asked.

"From under the car."

"In something?" Cassidy asked.

"There's a pan under the car," Lou said. "I was draining the engine."

Cassidy inhaled. "Bren, are you all right?"

Picking herself up, Bren assessed her scratches. "Yes. Are you?"

"We're going to have to get to the hospital."

"You're hurt?" Brenna grasped Cassidy's arm. At their feet, Ranger whimpered.

"No. I meant the vet," Cassidy said. "Ranger's gotten into the car fluids. They're poisonous."

Lou slapped his chest. "Don't accuse me. I was trying to get him out of it."

"I don't blame you," she replied sharply. Turning back to Brenna, she said, "I need to get going."

"Well, let's go then."

Gwen came out of the house. "Where are you going?"

"Taking Ranger to the vet," Cassidy explained.

"Do you need the ambulance?"

Cassidy shook her head. "Call and cancel it."

"No, damn it. I want someone to check out these bites," Lou said.

Brenna looked at the marks on his arms. None of the scratches, even a gouge or two, looked like they would need more than antiseptic and a band-aid. "Well, let's go."

"I want that dog checked for rabies," Lou demanded. "Look at him now. All fight then, now nothing."

Cassidy shook her head. "He's up on his shots. But I'll get you a full report."

"Let's go." Brenna turned around to summon the boys.

"Bren?"

"Yes?"

They started to walk to the Mountaineer. Ranger's lope was noticeably slower. Then he paused, panting and whining, before he lay down in the grass.

Leaning down to look at her pet, Cassidy said, "I need you to keep Ryan with you, Bren," Cassidy emphasized. "I don't know how this is going to come out."

Brenna looked down at the dog, who looked incapable of attacking anyone at the moment. "You don't want me there?" She looked up in time to see Lou stalking inside his home, ushering his children ahead of him.

"I don't want Ryan to deal with this. Please, Bren?"

"Are you sure you're alright?" She looked critically at Cassidy. The woman had taken a nasty fall in the pile of bodies. Brenna couldn't forget the life-threatening injuries only recently healed. "You need to rest. Thomas and I can take Ranger."

Cassidy inhaled, pressing a careful hand to her ribs. She pursed her lips, exhaled and then opened her eyes. "Do you understand that it'll hurt worse if I don't do this first?"

Their gazes met; Brenna relived in that moment the nightmare of her vigil at Cassidy's hospital bedside. She hadn't wanted to leave either, in case Cassidy took a bad turn and she wasn't there — only to pray, if nothing else. Ranger was an animal, but no less important to Cassidy and Ryan than another family member.

She could not say she understood it, having never owned a pet herself, but Cassidy needed to do this. And what Cassidy needed, Brenna wanted to give her. She nodded tersely, agreeing to the plan.

Holding Ryan's shoulders, they and James watched Cassidy and Thomas walk the rest of the way to the Mountaineer together, Ranger's steps faltering between them. Thomas said something to Cassidy. They stopped, and with no protest from Ranger, Thomas lifted the dog into his arms.

"What's up with the dog?" James asked. "Did he get hurt by Mr. Talbot?"

Brenna shook her head. Reaching down she took the tennis ball from Ryan's hands. "No. When no one was looking, Ranger went after this, which apparently was in the drain pan under the car."

James made a disgusted face.

"Where are Mommy and Thomas going with Ranger?" Ryan asked as they turned to the sidewalk. Thomas and Cassidy had laid Ranger in the back seat and were climbing into the Mountaineer's front seats.

"To Ranger's doctor to make sure he's okay," Brenna said. "We'll go back to your house to wait until they get back." Watching Ryan wipe his hands on his jeans, Brenna realized that he had gotten into the fluid pan himself. "Ryan, did you get any of that wet stuff in your mouth or eyes?"

He looked at his hands. "No."

"I think we'll still wash up when we get inside." Grasping Ryan's hand, she cautioned, "Just don't touch your face, okay?"

"Okay."

Following her inside the Hylands' home, James remarked, "Maybe we should have let Cassidy take the dog on the camping trip."

"I thought he would be too excitable. She needed rest, not to be dragged around by the dog."

"Next time we'll just deal," James suggested. "This is depressing."

Brenna had to agree this was a depressing way to end their first family vacation. She sent her prayers after Cassidy to the veterinarian's office.

"Which way?" Thomas's question drew Cassidy's gaze off Ranger laying quietly in the back seat.

"Turn left here, then a right when you get to Thornton, and it's in the Dantzinger Plaza."

"All right." Thomas pulled the Mountaineer out from the stop sign.

Directions given, Cassidy returned to her vigil over Ranger.

"Is he going to be okay?" Thomas asked.

While he didn't look terrible, he was far quieter than she was used to. "I don't know," she admitted.

"Is poison treatment the same for dogs as it is for humans?"

"What do you mean?"

"Well, for people either make them throw up, or give them lots of water to flush it through their system." Cassidy was openly surprised. Thomas elaborated sheepishly, "Survival stuff I learned."

Cassidy dipped her head in acknowledgment. Taking her mind willingly to this other topic, she asked, "Did you enjoy the program? What's it called?"

"FIRE. And, yeah, everything has been fantastic." He guided the SUV through another turn. "Here we are."

Turning off the engine, Thomas got out and opened the door to the back seat. "Ready to get fixed up, boy?"

Ranger chewed his hand though it didn't break the skin.

"Go ahead," Cassidy said, rubbing Ranger's hindquarters from the other open door.

Wrestling just a bit with lifting the medium-sized dog while Ranger didn't resist, Thomas finally got out of the car. Cassidy quickly closed all the doors to the vehicle and then led the way into the animal hospital.

The receptionist stood up, taking stock of the situation.

"Poison," Cassidy explained. They walked to the door which led to the exam rooms while the receptionist disappeared in another direction.

In the corridor, Cassidy spotted Dr. Davidson striding up. "He was poisoned?"

"Antifreeze we think. The neighbor was draining his into a pan Ranger drank from."

Taking a look at the dog, he stepped back out. "Stacy, bring me two IV bags, and the purgative."

Davidson began examining Ranger's eyes, nose, throat and palpating his abdomen. When his hand came away from Ranger's muzzle, he frowned and sniffed his fingers. "Yeah, that's antifreeze." What bothered Cassidy the most though was the fact that Ranger didn't react.

The vet tech, Stacy, reappeared and assisted with establishing the IV and recording vital signs. She reported, "His blood pressure's weak."

The vet took a look at the numbers himself and Cassidy questioned him when his expression turned grim. "What?"

"His body has been working hard. What was he doing?"

"Playing ball with some kids, and my neighbor was working on his car."

Nodding with understanding, Davidson turned back to Ranger. "He got thirsty. That antifreeze was too tempting, wasn't it, boy?" He rubbed Ranger's ears as he spoke to Cassidy. "We'll get him hydrated, flush his system." Just a step away from the exam table, he pulled open a cabinet and withdrew a bottle of dark pills.

"So what can be done for him?"

"The IV will bring his fluid levels up. We can't let his kidneys shut down. They're his body's natural cleaners." He held up the bottle and gave it a shake. "This charcoal will absorb the antifreeze. We'll see how it goes."

Cassidy sagged as Davidson easily coaxed Ranger to take down two of the pills.

"You can sit in here if you want to," Davidson offered. "But maybe you would rather..."

"Here's fine." Cassidy knew her response was too curt to be considered polite and sighed. Thomas came to Cassidy's shoulder and they both watched Ranger getting connected to a heart monitor and other equipment. The dog was quiet, fully supine against the exam table, and his eyes were closed.

She focused on Thomas' hand on her shoulder and the soft fur under her fingertips as she stroked Ranger's side.

"Anything I can do?" Thomas asked her.

"You should take your mom home. It's been a long day."

"She'll want to come here."

Rubbing Ranger between his ears, she kissed his neck. "I'll call Bren and make her understand."

"This is Mom," Thomas reminded her. "She leaped in when Ranger pulled you down."

Cassidy remembered that. "She did, didn't she?"

"Yeah. And she's not going to accept you going through this alone."

They stopped by the reception counter. Cassidy tapped on it. When the receptionist turned, Cassidy gestured to the phone, signaling her desire to use it. Respecting the silence, the woman nodded.

Dialing her home, Cassidy tried to figure out what to say to convince Brenna.

"Bren, please don't bring Ryan here," Cassidy pleaded. Standing at the reception desk, she leaned heavily on it and tiredly brushed the fingers of her left hand through her hair in exasperation. On the other end of the connection, she could hear Brenna's breathing to the point she sensed the other woman opening her mouth, readying another counter-proposal. It had been the same for the last ten minutes. She interrupted this time. "Things are quiet now. Nothing but waiting. Ryan is more comfortable at home."

"We can help him. He's five. It's part of life..."

"Puppies being born, maybe, but not this," Cassidy said. "Not suffering."

"Is Ranger really in pain?" Brenna asked, her voice quiet. "Maybe you should..."

"No!" Cassidy covered her face. *God, she did not want to face this.* The doctor, in and out of the exam room with Ranger, kept going and coming with test vials. "Not until I'm sure."

"Ryan knows hospitals help." Brenna pointed out, "He saw you."

Brenna had helped him through that.

"No." Her stomach grumbled, giving her another diversionary idea. "It's dinner time. Everyone needs to eat."

"I've already located dinner here for Ryan and James. You have Thomas with you. Want me to bring you something?"

Cassidy's back began throbbing in time with the ache in her

temples. Her doctor had warned her that exhaustion and aches would come more easily. She shifted her stance again and leaned against the wall. She saw the vet once again entering Ranger's exam room. "Bren, I have to go. I will send Thomas to you. Get everyone settled. I'll call you soon."

She hung up. Thomas looked at her in question. "You need to go," she said.

"Why?"

"Your mother needs to get everyone home."

"I'll come back here after that," he said. "You need someone to make you sit down. I know your back must be killing you."

"Your mother taught you too well," Cassidy remarked, but she did sit. Thomas sat next to her. Dr. Davidson emerged from the exam room again, a fresh vial in hand. Cassidy pushed to her feet. "Doctor?"

"Time for a stool and urine test," he said.

"Improvement?"

"Some. Let me get this started for analysis, and I'll be right back."

Finally shooing Thomas out to get his mother, brother, and Ryan home across town, Cassidy leaned forward tiredly in her chair. She let her gaze go distant and recalled acquiring Ranger.

The dog had been fifteen months old, the last of a litter where the rest had sold by the time they were all five months old. However, Ranger, bought twice, had escaped from each home and made his way back to the breeding farm in northern California. After the second time, where Ranger had left the buyer who lived in Oregon, the breeder had resigned himself to never getting this particular Dalmatian off his hands.

Following her permanent move to California and her divorce, Cassidy wanted a dog for Ryan as a companion. She chose to investigate a Dalmatian because it had a good reputation both for protection and with children. She had still feared Mitch then, and hoped to enhance her own sense of security at home with the dog.

She had looked at all the puppies of this breeder's most recent litter, questioning whether or not she had the time to adapt a puppy to her hectic lifestyle. Sitting on the floor among them, she had turned around to see Ryan, just barely three years old at the time, pulling at the ears of a muscular, full-grown Dalmatian. The breeder had been just as stymied.

Ranger, he said, seldom showed interest in the visitors who came looking for dogs. Yet the Dalmatian nosed Ryan, clearly tolerant of, and even enjoying, Ryan's attempts to climb onto his back.

Cassidy had taken Ranger home that day, the breeder's warning that the dog would probably run away ringing fresh in her ears. Each night, Ryan had to be dragged inside from playing with Ranger in the backyard well past dark. Each morning, Ranger stood at the sliding door looking for Ryan. He never did run away.

Hearing footsteps, Cassidy looked up. She followed the vet once again into the exam room. Rubbing Ranger's spotted coat as the vet opened the dog's mouth and swabbed his tongue, Cassidy saw Ranger's eyes were open and he seemed less dazed, following Davidson's hands around his face.

The vet then smiled and rubbed the top of Ranger's head. "Good boy," he encouraged.

Cassidy grew hopeful. "Good?"

"He should be good to go soon."

"He'll get better then?"

"He is underweight, and had just been highly active. Each thing alone wouldn't have been a problem. But all together... though I don't think he got more than a lick or two of the antifreeze."

"I thought he looked a little thin," Cassidy recalled. When the doctor tilted his head in a clear question, she explained, "He hasn't been in my care for the last two weeks." Pulling over a chair she sat down intending to make up for some of that lost time as she continued to stroke Ranger's fur. "My... partner and I... We took our sons camping."

Davidson left her and the dog alone. Cassidy rested her chin against her fist, encouraging Ranger to look at her as she talked to him about Ryan, watching his ears flicker at the name.

Brenna finished washing the dinner dishes, and then dried and put them away so nothing would remain out when they left Cassidy's home again. The garbage went directly to the big can in Cassidy's garage, and then Brenna walked the bin to the curb.

The trash service might not come for days, but she didn't want Cassidy to come home to a rancid smell. She'd leave a note for the lawn service to put the empty bin away when they came.

Brenna sighed, still smarting from Cassidy's anger on the phone. She had to remind herself that Cassidy handling her own business was not a rejection. She might not ask soon enough to suit Brenna, but it was Cassidy's right to choose when, where, and how she helped.

Not used to being unasked, Brenna was still trying to decide where and when she could offer help. The process of figuring out where the line lay had led not only to discussions, but deeply hurtful fights as well.

Since opening herself to listen when Cassidy spoke when they were repairing their professional relationship, Brenna heard every emotion in the younger woman's voice. Waves from each buffeted Brenna and she often reflected them back, getting just obstinate and stubborn. Not among her better qualities. Now in their intimacy, it was even more important to be circumspect.

When she realized she was digging in during their latest conversation, Brenna had finally sensed when to disengage.

She walked back inside the house. "Ryan! James!" Walking back to the bedrooms, she found Ryan on the floor with an album in his hands. "What's that?" she asked.

"Pictures of me and Ranger," Ryan answered.

"Do you want to take it with you?"

"We're going away again?"

"Just back to our house."

Ryan ran out of the room. Seconds later, she heard the front door open and close. Sighing, she collected the album.

James sat up on Ryan's bed. "Are we stopping by the vet office?"

"She doesn't want Ryan there," Brenna said. "I don't know that I agree, especially since he seems to be focusing on the dog." She indicated the album. "But she was adamant. I'll take the album and talk to her again tonight. Maybe we'll see Ranger tomorrow."

Just as they reached the living room, Thomas stepped in the front door.

"All set?" Thomas asked.

Brenna nodded, ushered James and Ryan out ahead of her and held Thomas back for a quick conversation. "How is Ranger?"

"Still holding his own when I left."

"Hope?"

"I don't know." Thomas shook his head.

"Well, let's get back to the house. Did you grab a business card?"

Thomas smiled faintly. "I knew you'd want to call her, whether or not she called you." He withdrew the card from his rear right jean pocket and passed it to her.

"Thank you."

Brenna pulled the door shut on the bedroom with the knob turned, until she could release it without much sound. Pressing her hand tenderly to the door she silently wished Ryan a quiet night's sleep. Finally, she walked to the master bedroom for her own evening to start.

It had taken nearly an hour, the time now pushing nine-thirty, to convince Ryan to abandon his determined effort to construct a dog replica using his reacquired Legos. Brenna looked at the vet's business card.

She was worried about that actually. Ryan had fixated on Ranger, but he was not talking about his feelings. Brenna had to accept Cassidy knew her son best. Her insistence about keeping Ryan away had to be respected, despite the fact that Brenna would have chosen to handle things differently.

With a heavy heart, Brenna undressed. She was unsure she would ever get this relationship thing right. Stepping into the bathroom she pulled on a lacy white cotton nightgown. Then she sat at her vanity and brushed out her hair. Her unsmiling reflection and gunmetal tint to her eyes made her pause. She looked over to the phone on the bedside table. Cassidy still had not called. Standing she pulled on the cotton robe hanging over the back of the chair, smelling Cassidy's scent in the fabric and hugging it close to her body. She sat down on the bed and picked up the phone, pausing mid-dial to put it back in its cradle.

She has to handle this how she sees fit and I need to respect that. Finally she took her eyes off of the phone and stretched out on the bed. Bending forward over her outstretched legs, she grasped her feet and massaged them.

Still, she pleaded silently with Cassidy to call, to give her some news, ideas for what to do about Ryan, or just ask for help.

Closing her eyes, Brenna crossed her hands in her lap, needing to let go of the frustration. She reminded herself, *Love her enough to let her do this her way.*

"Are you praying?"

Brenna opened her eyes and saw Ryan in his fitted pajamas covered with cartoon drawings of bunnies and beavers. He was standing at the door, still holding the knob. "What is it, Ryan?"

He hesitated; she gestured for him to join her on the bed.

Watching Ryan climb onto the bed drew Brenna back ten years when her sons had been young and full of questions. He wrapped his small arms around her throat and head tightly, pressing his head against hers.

His small body felt quite tense and she rubbed his back before she helped him arrange himself against the other pillows and tuck his feet under the top edge of the covers. His gaze remained fixed on her. She asked lightly, "Now that you're settled, what can I do for you?"

"Were you praying?" he asked again.

It hadn't been formal prayer. However, she had been seeking strength and understanding, and calm from somewhere. "Yes, I was."

He looked at his own hands and folded them together in his lap as he had seen her do. After a moment like that, he bit his lower lip. "Will you show me how?"

The question startled Brenna. As far as she knew Cassidy and Ryan didn't attend a church. Brenna couldn't recall specifically discussing religious beliefs with Cassidy. As for herself, she had been raised Roman Catholic but fallen away from the rituals over the years. Cassidy's parents were regular churchgoers, though the denomination seemingly had encouraged them to spurn their own daughter and they hadn't been in contact since leaving Cassidy's hospital room in February.

Clearly Ryan was looking for a way to address his feelings. She proceeded carefully. "Is there something you want to pray for?" she asked.

"Ranger. He's sick. I want him to get well."

Cupping the boy's hands in her own, Brenna pressed them with light reassurance. "Whenever you wish, God listens." This she could say with utter confidence.

"To me?"

"Especially to you."

"But I wish all the time, and I get all my candles on the first blow. And none of them ever come true. Bad things just keep happening."

How deep is he going with this? "What sort of bad things are you thinking of?" she asked.

"I always wished my mom and dad would live together again. But that doesn't happen. My dad hit my mom. Grandpa hit her. I wished they would stop, but they didn't. Wishing isn't praying.

Because I wish and nothing happens. God didn't make them stop. Praying has to be different. It has to be stronger."

Brenna was stymied. If she said praying could make bad things stop happening, and Ranger didn't come home, Ryan would likely never believe her about anything ever again. She wrapped her arms around Ryan and kissed the top of his head. "Praying is still like wishing," she said, thinking carefully. "But it's more like asking for help to understand why certain things are happening. And for a way to help it stop happening."

Ryan studied his hands putting them together and then parting them several times. Anxiously he looked up at her. "But what if I do it wrong? God will punish me, and Ranger will never come home."

"You can't pray wrong," Brenna said. "The veterinarian is the person with the knowledge to help Ranger. You can ask God to help him be as smart as possible so he can help Ranger in the best way."

"What words do I say?"

"What words do you want to say?"

Ryan looked thoughtfully at his hands, folding and unfolding his fingers around each other. "Just say them?"

Brenna nodded and Ryan closed his eyes.

"Dear God," he said. "Ms. Lanigan says I can just talk to you." Brenna smiled. "I love Ranger a whole lot. He got sick today. Mommy took him to the hospital, like when she went. Can you make sure that his doctor is as smart as the one who healed Mommy?" Ryan paused and opened his eyes, looking up at Brenna, his expression serious. "You have to pray too. I know God listens to you."

Swallowing down the lump in her throat, Brenna dutifully closed her eyes, and folded her hands together. "Dear God, Ranger has been a wonderful friend to Ryan. Today, Ranger needs a friend and we hope you can be there for him, and make him happy again."

Ryan looked at her strangely. However, Brenna could not outright pray for Ranger to come home. Happiness she could explain, even if the dog died. Even Ryan's choice of asking to make the doctor as smart as his mother's had been could be explained if Ranger had to be put to sleep. If Ranger didn't come home though, there would be no explaining why her prayer did not work.

"Was that a prayer?" the boy asked.

Brenna nodded. When the silence lengthened, she asked, "Can you go to sleep now?"

"Can I stay here?"

"I have to read some things for my work," she said, retrieving the movie script from the bedside table.

"Mommy did that a lot too. I learned how to sleep with the light on," Ryan said, sounding serious.

Brenna smiled at his earnestness, a plain need to be able to stay with her evident. She nodded. "Lay down then."

Laying down so his back rested against Brenna's hip, Ryan scooted further under the covers. She removed one pillow so he laid flatter, and stroked his shoulder before she pulled the cover over it.

"Good night."

"Sleep well, Ryan."

Brenna had just reached the last scene of the script when the noise of an engine shifting into idle made her look up to see the faint glow of headlights hitting her window. A moment later, she heard the front door open. She looked at the clock and saw it was past midnight.

She waited as the footsteps neared, knowing who it was, but not wanting to rush whatever news Cassidy might have, good or bad.

Her lover's blonde head hung down and her shoulders slumped when she appeared at the doorway. Her hair was loose, hiding her face from immediate scrutiny.

"Cass?" Brenna saw her eyes were wet, her expression haggard. She looked away to Ryan still sleeping, suddenly certain he shouldn't hear. "Do you want to talk somewhere else?" she asked quietly.

Shaking her head, Cassidy lowered herself to the mattress. "I'm worn out," she said. Her voice sounded raspy and raw.

Brenna bit the bullet and asked, "And Ranger?"

Cassidy's expression brightened as she lifted her head. "The worst is over," she said. "Dr. Davidson says he'll be fine. He's keeping him in their kennel to bring up his body weight and keep him better hydrated."

Relief flooded every muscle in Brenna's body, making her lightheaded. She now understood how Cassidy could look so worn, despite good news. "Ryan prayed for that tonight," she said.

"He did?" Cassidy stood again and pulled off her shoes before stretching again on the bed. Ryan remained sleeping between them. Brenna watched her exhale and her shoulders visibly dropped their tension.

Brenna added, "He asked me to help."

"Did you?"

"I did." She brushed her fingers through Ryan's hair. "He was trying to make dogs out of the Legos tonight. I knew Ranger being sick bothered him, but until he came in here, he hadn't said a word about how he was feeling."

Cassidy nodded. "Thank you for taking care of him."

"You were busy." Brenna watched Cassidy inhale, obviously in pain again. "It was bad for a long time, wasn't it?"

"That's why I didn't call," Cassidy explained and apologized at the same time. "I was never sure what would be too much or not enough to say, and I didn't want to face Ryan if Ranger suddenly took a bad turn."

Brenna caught Ryan's movement. Their voices were waking him up. "Let me put him back to bed."

Cassidy shook her head. "It's all right." Ryan woke at her voice and his eyes met his mother's. "Hi, Ryan," she said softly.

"Mommy?" he questioned tiredly. "You're home."

Cassidy looked up at Brenna. "Yes, I'm home," she said. "And I have good news," she added. "Ranger is getting better."

Ryan rolled onto his back and Brenna was surprised he addressed her. "Thank you," he said.

"For what?"

"For praying for Ranger with me."

"You prayed for Ranger?" Despite Brenna already telling her that, Cassidy obviously wanted to hear it from Ryan's perspective.

"I couldn't sleep," Ryan said. "I came in and I found Ms. Lanigan praying." He sat up; everyone rearranged on the bed. "I asked her to show me how. She did." He smiled broadly, clearly proud of his accomplishment. "So I did. Now Ranger's better."

"Yes, he is," Cassidy confirmed.

"Can I see him?"

"It's late. You should be asleep."

"Can I see him tomorrow?" Ryan asked.

Cassidy explained, "He has to stay in the hospital for a few days. But I'm sure Ranger would like to see you."

"How do you know?" Ryan asked.

"I asked him," Cassidy said plainly.

"Ranger can't talk," Ryan countered.

"He certainly can in his own way," Cassidy said. "Now, if you go to bed, Brenna and I can figure out when you two get some time together so Ranger can say thank you for your prayers."

Ryan smiled. Cassidy brushed her fingers through his hair and kissed his cheek. He climbed over her, and off the bed.

Standing in the doorway, he looked back. "Good night, Mommy. Ms... Brenna."

"Ryan," Brenna sounded surprised to be called by her first name. Cassidy grasped her hand.

"Good night, Ryan," the two women said in unison.

"Should he call me by my first name?" Brenna asked.

"I think it'll be alright," Cassidy explained. "I call you Brenna, and I love you, so he's chosen to show his love for you that way, too."

She looked at the door her son had carefully closed. "Ranger's attachment to Ryan is just as strong," she said as she stood and undressed. "He responded each time I mentioned Ryan to him."

"James may be right. Next time we go camping, we should take Ranger with us."

"I'd like that." When Cassidy returned to the bed, Brenna brushed her fingers over the woman's wan, washed features.

"You need some sleep," Brenna said. "Come here."

Cassidy conceded readily, lowering herself to the mattress, allowing herself to be wrapped up in Brenna's arms. She rested her head on her partner's breast and put her own right arm across Brenna's stomach. Once they were skin to skin, she felt all the tension pulled from her body and soon was fast asleep.

GALWAY GETAWAY

County Clare, Ireland
July 2001

"HERE."

Cassidy Hyland turned in the wood chair she had commandeered on the cottage's small concrete patch outside the back door. She took the ale bottle her lover Brenna Lanigan held toward her. Looking at the label, she asked, "Should we be drinking?"

"Everyone's turned in early. Apparently a long day of intercontinental travel kills even the hardiest 'I want to experience the night life' teen plans." Brenna chuckled.

Watching her lover settle into the other chair on the porch, Cassidy was taken anew at how good the auburn-haired woman looked "out of uniform" wearing a shrub-green airy button-up blouse, and matching knee-length shorts with a tan belt.

Until three months ago they had been acting on the same television program, *Time Trails*, where a pseudo-military style had dictated their on-camera wardrobe. But now that the series was a wrap, it seemed Brenna's true style had emerged in her choices of clothing. For the hours-long flight across North America from LAX to New York's JFK airport, they had agreed paparazzi cameras might catch them, so they dressed in casual chic: slacks and airy blouses. That had been handy as their new family – Cassidy, Brenna, and their three sons, Ryan, James and Thomas – were photographed several times, though approached for statements only once.

She smiled as she recalled Brenna's response: "My family is taking a vacation to Ireland. Afterward I will be filming a new movie."

Family. Reaching across the space to cover the woman's hand on the arm of her chair, she lifted her ale in her other hand. "A toast," she suggested.

"To what?" Brenna leaned forward and clicked the neck of her bottle to Cassidy's.

"To the official start of family vacation."

Brenna chuckled. "I'll drink to that." She took a long swig of her ale. "Oh," she exclaimed. "That hits the spot." Her hand shifted under Cassidy's and soon their fingers were threaded together. "How are you doing?"

"I'm not quite as tired as the kids," Cassidy admitted. "My brain is buzzing though. Is it possible to be too tired to sleep?"

"Too wired. Same thing happened to me on late night shoots," Brenna said.

"Do you think you'll have many on the movie?" Cassidy asked.

"There's about two dozen night scenes in the script. If it stays intact, I'm in five of them."

"That's not too bad."

"It's going to make phone calls home difficult," Brenna said.

"How so?" Cassidy sipped on her ale.

"As I tucked him in, Ryan asked what time it was." Brenna shifted in her chair. "The face clock on the bedside table showed seven-fifteen."

"He told you that was too early," Cassidy guessed. Her son, age five (five-and-a-half, he'd tell her), had an eight-thirty bedtime, though during the summer months, she often let him stay up until nine.

Brenna nodded. "He remembered though that we had left LA at nine-thirty and asked how we had gone backward in time. I told him we hadn't. I figured out the time difference and pointed out it was eleven in the morning back home."

Home. Cassidy looked down at their joined hands. She looked up into Brenna's gaze and tugged lightly.

"Hmm?" Brenna asked.

"Come sit here," she said. She glanced over the rolling hills visible from their rented bed and breakfast. "It's a nice view."

"I can see that."

She rolled her eyes a little and the smirk on Brenna's face told her she'd understood the invitation. Then Brenna hid her lips behind her bottle and finished it off in one long swallow.

Keeping hold of Cassidy's hand as she stood up, Brenna put down the bottle on the small wood table between their chairs. "You finished?"

Cassidy tipped her head back and swallowed the remains of her bottle. Slim fingers wound around hers and extricated the brown glass from her hand. "Hmm?" Now it was her turn for a question.

"Just clearing away the breakables," Brenna said, setting it down next to her own empty one.

"I see."

Patting her knees, Cassidy welcomed her lover sideways onto her lap. When Brenna cupped her cheek, she leaned into their kiss and held the woman's hips securely.

Brenna's arms slipped around Cassidy's back and her fingers slid up into her hair, gently massaging the base of her neck. "Mm," she murmured agreeably and indulged herself in the taste of Brenna's lips and tongue.

Her own hands navigated up Brenna's back, squeezing muscles through her blouse. Passion rising, she wanted to feel the woman's naked skin.

Brenna eased back from their kiss; she was breathing hard. "Let's take a walk."

"Right now? I had other ideas." From the way Brenna's pupils had widened, Cassidy knew the other woman had the same ideas.

"But I want to *jump* you." Brenna blushed following her lust-filled words. "So, I have to bleed off some of this adrenaline."

"Are you thinking I won't consent to being ravished by a red-headed Celtic goddess on the Irish moors?" Cassidy teased. That was the role that Brenna had been cast in a magical fantasy she would start filming in a week.

"Oh, god."

"Goddess," Cassidy replied. Both of them laughed. "All right, my goddess, let's take that walk."

Hand in hand, they stepped away from the house onto a

stepping stone path that wound around the property. The moon was full and the sky was exceptionally clear compared to Los Angeles. The difference between city and country, Cassidy thought. And this was very, very beautiful country.

As she stroked her thumb over the side of Brenna's hand in hers she studied the rented house. Technically a cottage, flower gardens hugged its walls. A large vegetable garden, filled with stakes climbed by vines and mounds covered in short green leaves, had been boxed out at a distance from the house. A short stacked-stone wall followed the dips and rises along the edge of the property. Beyond lay hills dappled with moonlight and it looked like there was a flock of sheep in the distance.

They had crossed paths with a flock on the highway coming down from Galway. The shepherd had carried a gnarled stick and held the gate open while a dog herded the animals along the path. It had briefly made Cassidy feel like she'd stepped onto the set of "The Quiet Man" or "Brigadoon."

Cassidy turned to look at Brenna, smiling as moonlight brightened the reds in her hair. Her lover's face was relaxed, the moonlight illuminating her blue eyes. Her fingers clung to Cassidy's. She pressed a kiss to Brenna's cheek.

"Hmm?" Brenna mused, turning her head, gaze meeting Cassidy's. So Cassidy kissed her deeply, pulling the smaller woman's body into her own. "Mm hmm." Brenna threaded her fingers through Cassidy's hair.

When they finally gave up for breath, Cassidy said quietly, "You fit here."

"Thank you for coming with me."

After nuzzling Brenna's nose, Cassidy said, "That's what family does."

She returned them to walking the path, content in the silence broken occasionally by the bleat of a lamb drifting across the hills. When they had finished walking the property, they returned to the porch, gathered up their bottles, and went back inside the cottage.

Brenna moved around the cottage's first floor, shutting off many of the lights and lamps. She turned the deadbolts on the front and rear doors to the cottage and closed a couple curtains. Dropping their empty ale bottles into the trash can in the latching cupboard beside the sink, she finally moved toward the master bedroom where she could faintly hear Cassidy moving about. The boys had been given the entire second floor, two bedrooms around a shared bathroom. She and Cassidy were alone here on the first floor. She knocked on the master bedroom door.

Cassidy opened it. "You don't have to knock." She kissed Brenna and drew her into the room, closing them together in the space. The bedroom was significantly smaller than a hotel room in the States and the bathroom–*water closet*, she corrected–was the actual size of a closet, she noted when she saw the small door to the right of a squat double dresser. A moderately sized mirror had been mounted on the wall above the dresser, giving her a view behind her to watch Cassidy pulling back the sheets on their bed.

"I guess I'm used to hiding our bedroom from the boys," Brenna said. "I wasn't sure if you were already undressed."

Cassidy wasn't, at least not completely. Her blonde hair flowed over her shoulders and her blouse was unbuttoned, though the sides tenuously held to her ample chest, hiding her nipples from view. She'd obviously pulled the blouse back on after removing her bra, which told Brenna that Cassidy also had been thinking about modesty when she heard the knock.

Black slacks that the blonde had worn all day traveling were now folded over a straight-back chair next to a small table with another mirror. Her bikini cut underwear showed off her long legs, which made up much of the woman's height, several inches taller than Brenna. Brenna's heart beat faster as she thought about tangling her own with them.

She hadn't been lying about wanting to jump her blonde lover. But the idea of doing so had felt wrong. It had seemed only right to take her passion down a notch until she could get it under control. It simmered now, warming her belly.

Unbuttoning her blouse and shorts, Brenna set them on the dresser. Going through her bag next to the pile, she searched for her toiletries. Warm fingers slid over her shoulders. Lifting her gaze, she found Cassidy's gaze holding hers. The woman stood behind her and deftly removed her bra.

"The house is cozy enough to go with a nightgown," Cassidy stated. "Considering how far north we are, I'm surprised. I had packed for cold nights."

"Does that mean you don't have *anything* to wear to bed?" Brenna asked, her voice dropping seductively. Turning, she slid her arms around Cassidy's waist inside the shirt and kissed the space between her breasts.

Cassidy's hands sifted into Brenna's hair. She inhaled from the pleasure that already throbbed in her center. She was wet and... Full lips touched her ear and seductively whispered, "It means we can wear *nothing* to bed."

"God," Brenna whispered as Cassidy's lips covered hers. The movement of her lover's mouth was intense and coaxing, passionate. Cassidy's tongue pressed inside her parted lips; she didn't try to control her moan. There were definite benefits to the boys being asleep an entire floor away.

When Cassidy drew her to the bed, Brenna took in the several colorful quilts and crisp white sheets already pulled back. Her knees bumped the mattress and she stumbled. As she straightened, Cassidy's hands found her calves. The other woman removed her shoes and massaged her feet, causing another pleased moan to fall from her lips.

"Come here," she breathed, reaching out and beckoning to her lover.

Shrugging her shoulders, Cassidy dropped her blouse to the floor before she climbed onto the bed, sliding her knees along the outside of Brenna's hips. Her blonde hair a halo around her head, Cassidy leaned forward and pressed Brenna to the sheets with sure hands. Stroking her fingers through Brenna's hair, she said softly, "This feels like our first time."

"It is our first time... *in Ireland*," Brenna agreed.

Cassidy laughed. The sound slipped along Brenna's nerves and sang in her blood. Hungry passion rose once again.

Wrapping her arms around the woman's neck, Brenna pulled her down until their breasts were pillowed together and she felt the other woman's heart beating against hers. "Ye are a big bonnie lass," she said, pushing forward the brogue she had been working on with the voice coach for the film. "N I aim t' make luv t' ye fer 'ours."

Cassidy's eyes, normally ice blue, went dark as the night sky outside, filled with raw lust. "God, that's perfect." The depths of her lover's voice increased Brenna's passion. She closed her lips over Cassidy's pulse point and sucked softly. A desperately impassioned groan echoed in her ear. She parted her legs, moved her hands down along a sinuously muscled back, and massaged Cassidy's ass, guiding the woman's heated center against her own.

When Cassidy pushed up on her hands, her hips shifted, which pressed their sexes tightly together. Brenna clutched at Cassidy's back, half-lifting herself from the bed, caught up in the delight of their skin's touch everywhere. Moving her lips over Cassidy's breasts, she latched onto a hardened nipple. The gasp above her head and the flood of moist heat against her belly told her she had given Cassidy exactly what she needed.

Everything but Cassidy then fell away from her awareness. She filled herself up instead on Cassidy's every shift, shudder, and sigh, determined to bring Cassidy as much pleasure as possible. Sucking on a nipple, she massaged the taut muscles of the woman's back and ass. Cassidy orgasmed with a cry, hips jerking sharply against Brenna's upraised knee, then collapsed against her.

Brenna nibbled and kissed her lover's jaw and throat. Moving her thigh a little, she enjoyed the sight of Cassidy again rocking on it. Her moisture spread across Brenna's skin. A moment later, Cassidy gasped several times and arched in her second orgasm.

Kissing Cassidy's cheek and caressing the high color, Brenna let Cassidy move off to the side. She watched her panting, soothing her fingers over the woman's shoulder. Finally, she brushed locks of hair off Cassidy's face and gently kissed her nose.

Finally she sat up. Cassidy's hand tiredly caressed her back as she arranged the sheet and one of the blankets over them. At last, Brenna cuddled back in with her lover, hummed in happiness, and closed her eyes.

Feeling warm and heavy, Cassidy slowly blinked opened her eyes and shifted her nose deeper into Brenna's hair. She took a deep breath and remembered going to sleep curled into Brenna. At some point their positions had reversed and she'd become the big spoon. Flexing her hands, she recognized a soft breast under her fingers and shifted her fingers around it, lightly squeezing. As she did, Brenna stretched and the small mound filled Cassidy's palm. She smirked and kissed the woman's upraised naked shoulder.

"Mm," Brenna hummed. Rolling onto her back, her gaze met Cassidy's, eyes blue as wildflowers. "Good morning," was issued throatily and sounded insanely seductive.

"Good morning," she replied. Closing her eyes, she slid her lips over Brenna's, kissing her tenderly. She was in no rush to leave this room or this bed right away.

Brenna's hip rested against her belly and nearly all the woman's body was within easy reach. Cassidy slipped her hand from breast to belly, and further, to the tidy thatch of hair over Brenna's sex. She nipped at Brenna's lips. "Open up," she coaxed.

Legs parted and while kissing her lover, Cassidy massaged Brenna's core until it was throbbing and wet. For long languorous moments she continued their kiss, listening to Brenna's breathing become faster and shallower. Shifting her fingers, she used her thumb on Brenna's clit until her lover had to tear her mouth away with a gasping cry, hips jerking. "Cass!"

Grinning, Cassidy reclaimed Brenna's lips with a final kiss and eased her fingers from Brenna's tight and soaked center. She indulged in licking her fingers clean of the woman's taste.

"God," Brenna panted, her eyes unfocused. She reverently held Cassidy's cheeks, focusing her gaze. "I'd ask how you slept, but you seem refreshed."

"And now, I'm hungry." She kissed Brenna's lips, letting the woman taste herself, then she moved down, pulling the sheet with her. As Brenna's fingers feathered through her hair, Cassidy licked at damp inner thighs and then settled into feast. Strong fingers gripped her left shoulder as Brenna clamped her other hand over her mouth to quiet her rising moans. Cassidy pushed her tongue deeper still, used her fingers to caress thick, puffy folds, and consumed the woman's essence.

Brenna gasped, catching her breath, and then she giggled when Cassidy, nipping her way upward, caught several ticklish spots. "Oh, dear God." Brenna panted while Cassidy nuzzled her ear.

Easing over to Brenna's side, Cassidy linked their ankles. She stroked her fingers through Brenna's hair and brushed it aside so she could drink in the woman's flushed and freshly fucked expression.

Slowly the woman regained her wits. After kissing Cassidy tenderly, Brenna said, "Let's see what this kitchen has in the way of breakfast."

Brenna leaned back against the kitchen counter, which felt like something out of the 1970s from the States. Drying her hands with a dish towel, she looked over the small alcove table filled with three boys. With varying degrees of enthusiasm they were eating the hash she had made from crumbled sausage, mixing it with eggs and shredded potatoes in a tureen-sized cast-iron skillet. Cassidy had doled out five glasses of a fruit juice she'd found in the refrigerator. Currently her lover was pouring coffee from a French press for the two of them.

Once her hands were dry, Brenna kissed the top of five-year-old

Ryan's blond hair before picking up a plate and scooping a serving of the hash onto it and sitting down at the nearest empty chair. A moment later Cassidy placed a steaming mug of coffee in front of her and sat down in another empty chair next to Thomas, Brenna's 18-year-old son, and across the table from her. James, Brenna's 16-year-old, sat at the far end looking still half-asleep as he poked at his dish.

"Eat up," Brenna said aloud. "We're going to a castle today."

Ryan started eating quickly. She slowed him down with a gentle hand over his rising spoon.

James looked up. "But what abou–?"

"It won't be all day. Probably just take the morning," Brenna said. "The school tours only take a couple hours."

"Thanks for breakfast," Thomas said, finishing his hash and his juice. "May I be excused?"

"Shower?" Brenna asked. He nodded. "Go ahead."

Ryan started to slide out of his chair.

"Ryan, where are you going?" Cassidy asked.

"Shower," he replied.

"Thomas is showering. You bathed last night. We'll go up to dress when you're finished," Cassidy said.

Brenna brushed her fingers through Ryan's hair. He had become quite attached to her elder son. She wondered if that would cause problems when Thomas went off to FIRE camp in August. Then she remembered. She would be here in Ireland filming while all that happened; Cassidy would be handling their children all on her own.

Ryan went back to scooping his hash, and finished quickly, though Cassidy was only a couple bites behind him. Brenna gathered their plates and glasses and kissed Cassidy when she stepped up to Ryan's chair to lead him upstairs.

"Let's go, Ryan." Cassidy coaxed her son from his chair. "Say thank you to Brenna."

Once he was on the floor, Ryan hugged Brenna, his head tucking tightly into her stomach as he tried to reach his arms all the way around her. He pulled back after a moment and looked up at her with a puckish smile. "Thank you."

"Did you enjoy it?" Brenna asked, cupping his chin and brushing his cheek with her thumb.

"Mm mm! Good!" He rubbed his stomach with one hand moving in a big circle and then broke away from her and ran to the stairs.

Cassidy touched Brenna's arm before she had fully turned away to the sink. "What's wrong?"

"I was just thinking... you're going to be the only one they have for a month."

"I've been a single mom for years. At least Ryan didn't pout this time. I think he'll be fine."

"All right." She accepted the blonde's kiss and then nodded toward the stairs. Ryan was working his way up rather quickly. "Better catch him before he interrupts Thomas."

Cassidy's long legs ate up the distance. She scooped Ryan into her arms halfway up the staircase, tickling him and making him laugh.

Turning to put the dishes in the sink and starting the water, Brenna heard James speak. "Do you think I can drive the car?"

She turned to look at her younger son still sitting at the table. James had just acquired his driver's license and asked frequently to drive anywhere and everywhere. She said reasonably, "The roads here are unfamiliar and many rules are different."

"But I learned to drive in the city." He frowned. "There's nothing here for miles."

"Kilometers," she corrected with a smile. His brows pinched and she relented. "We'll find a place you can do so, safely. But right now, I don't really know what sort of conditions we'll see."

He appeared to roll that around, his gaze diverting. Finally he nodded. "All right. Maybe I can drive myself to the art class?"

"We'll look over the maps together when we get back, all right?"

"Thanks, Mom." James stood and brought her his plate, silverware and glass. Growing fast, he topped her now by a couple inches so she had to tilt her head up to meet his eyes.

She recalled the first time she'd told Cassidy about James, her little runaway, whom she always found half a block away exploring someone else's yard, meeting a neighbor's dog, or digging holes in someone else's sandbox looking for treasure.

"I promise you can explore, but for my peace of mind, please, there's plenty of wild within walking distance, too, all right?"

He grinned and kissed her cheek. "Love you."

"I love you too."

Her gaze followed his progress up the stairs.

"Craggaunowen castle was built in 1550 by my ancestor John MacSioda MacNamara. It was ruined by Cromwell's forces and the family driven away. But some family members returned in the 1800s and began restoration..." A man dressed in the clan colors and wearing a scabbard on a wide belt, led them through the public areas of the castle, essentially an open-air museum. He had introduced himself as Connor Studdart.

Cassidy listened to the history of the castle with one ear, more interested in keeping her son's hands to himself until they were given permission to touch.

"John Hunt restored the castle fully in the 1960s," Connor said. "And we've hosted several archaeological digs in the Crannog. What they find they document and bring here to the displays."

The castle's center held display cases of various lengths and widths. Inside were Bronze age tools used in the kitchen, farming, and defense.

He led them over to a rough-hewn wooden structure. "Now, what would you boys like to see demonstrated first?"

Ryan reached for the scabbard on the man's hip. "No," she said, tugging him back.

"It's all right. I have someone who can help me demonstrate some fighting later," Connor said. "But for now, how about we try a hand thresher. It separates grains from the stalk."

Cassidy let Ryan go to their guide and watched his excitement as a few stalks were brought out of a bin and he demonstrated the technique. Just as Ryan was brought to the man's lap to try it himself, she felt Brenna's hand caress lightly against her back. "He's having fun."

She looked across her shoulder to see Brenna watching her son with a soft smile. "Yeah."

She spotted Thomas and James talking over another display. She strained to see and hear what the teens were discussing.

James was explaining, "They created pigments from different sources, crushed flowers, clay, and herbs and usually mixed it with oil or melted animal fats to paint with."

Thomas was smiling. "Nerd."

"Art's been everywhere since the first cave paintings," James replied, sounding put upon.

Thomas walked back to another display case and tapped on the glass. "Yeah, but seafaring, trapping, hunting, though, that's the stories the paintings told."

"I hope the art workshop will show us how some of the old pigments were made," James said.

Thomas shook his head, but threw a friendly arm over his brother's shoulder as they were ushered into another area. "Like I said..." He ruffled his brother's hair. "Nerd."

All of them got a chance to be hands-on when they were led to the stock pen and barn. Sheep, chickens, and a few geese and ducks cluttered a pecking yard next to a barn enclosure with a pair of cows. Ryan learned how to throw seed and collect eggs and Thomas and James took turns at shearing. Brenna gamely rolled up her sleeves, settled on a stool, and tried to follow their guide's example to milk the cow.

Connor stepped back and Brenna grimaced as she closed her hands around two of the thick teats. The texture was very leathery. The cow's tail flicked at her head, briefly catching her hair, then it shifted on its legs. She bit her lip and tried to recall how the position of Mr. Studdart's hands had gone.

A few awkward squirts into the process, Brenna growled low. As she tried to find the right combination of squeezing and stroking, she heard a low chuckle and looked over to see Cassidy's eyes twinkling, hiding her mouth behind her fingers. Brenna leaned back and planted her hands on her thighs. Meeting her lover's gaze, she smirked and then lifted one hand, curling her forefinger in a come-here gesture.

Calming a goose with strokes across its back so Ryan could get the egg, Thomas chuckled. "Watch out, Cass," he said. "She's competitive, remember."

Cassidy stepped closer to Brenna and crouched. "Show me what to do."

"You mean this?" Brenna grasped the teat on the cow's udder and gave it a proper stroking squeeze, having finally figured out the technique. A thick stream of milk arced toward Cassidy.

Backing up, the milk missed her, but Cassidy fell backward on her rear end.

"Oh no!" Brenna's frustration immediately fled, replaced with concern. She stood and reached out to help Cassidy up.

"I'm fine." Cassidy waved it away. "Got it. No teasing the Irish woman who can't milk an Irish cow."

"Ha ha." Cassidy gave her a kiss, improving her mood even

more. She gestured at the stool. "Give it a shot."

Ryan ran over when he saw his mother sit down. "Mommy," he said, holding up an egg, "you get milk to go with my egg so we have lunch."

Brenna grasped him under his arms, hoping he didn't drop the egg. "Just watch."

The pail beneath the cow dinged with the sound of a few successful squirts of milk. After a moment, Cassidy sat back and waved her son toward her. "Ryan, come see."

Taking the egg gingerly from Ryan's hands, Brenna handed it off to James, who was walking over from where he had been leaning on the fence railing. They all watched Ryan look down into the pail. He straightened up and shook his head. "Mommy, it's not white."

"True. There's a lot of fat, so it's not as white as what we get from the store," Cassidy explained. "It gets processed, cleaned up, and then they fortify it."

"What's fortify?" Ryan asked.

"Things are added to it," Brenna said. "To make it healthier so you can drink it to be strong."

Ryan flexed both arms, proudly showing off tiny muscles. "I'm strong."

"Because you drink your milk, kid." James laughed.

Transferring Ryan to her, Brenna met Cassidy's gaze. She was beginning to regret that she would not return to the States with them at the end of the week. She knew she had work, and it was good work, but this feeling that their little family was beginning to gel... She sighed. She didn't want to miss a minute of it.

"You have a wonderful place here. Thank you for the tour," she said. Her sons echoed her and Ryan waved.

"Enjoy the rest of your stay," Connor replied, waving at them from the entrance as they walked to the car.

"Mom, can I drive?"

"All right," Brenna said.

Cassidy nodded and walked over to James with the car key. "It's only a dozen kilometers back to the restaurant we saw on the road here." While Brenna followed Ryan into the back seat from one side and Thomas entered from the other, she told James, "It's definitely past time for lunch."

Brenna's younger son beamed at her and eagerly got into the car. Cassidy watched him check the seat position, the rearview mirror angle, and all the dashboard dials as he slid the key into the ignition. He tested the difference between the turn signal and activating the wipers.

"Everyone have their seatbelts on?" Cassidy asked.

"All set," Thomas said.

"All set," Ryan said from the back middle seat.

"Ready," Brenna replied. Cassidy watched her put her hand lightly on James's shoulder and squeeze. "Careful."

They only encountered two other cars going in the opposite direction as they headed back toward the main part of Quin, the town near Craggaunowen. Though a light rain had begun to fall, the pub was easy to spot with its scalloped windows. A sign out front proclaimed it The Monk's Well Inn. James found a space in the parking lot next to the building.

Stepping out he handed the keys to Brenna. "Thanks."

"Thank you," she replied.

Inside they were greeted by a smiling young woman. The group was led to a large polished hardwood table with seats for six. Everyone settled quickly.

The rain outside became heavier, pelting the building, and the wind whistled past the windows. "Just made it," Brenna said. "Hopefully it'll let up by the time we're done with lunch."

"Or we can hang out," Cassidy said. "This is our first chance to really check out an Irish pub."

"D'ye want spirits, beer, or wine?" the young woman asked, looking from the women to Thomas.

"He's only 18," Brenna said quickly.

"18 can drink. Also 16 and up with a parent's permission," the young woman replied. Thomas shook his head, declining the alcohol.

But James looked up, his expression clearly intrigued. "Really?"

Brenna shook her head. "If you drink, you can't drive the rest of the way to the cottage."

"Just a sip?" James asked.

Brenna pursed her lips. "Can we see what you have that doesn't have alcohol?"

"I'll be right back with the full menu."

Looking around the pub, Cassidy saw a pair of dartboards. "There's darts here."

"Do you play?" Thomas asked her. His gaze, blue like his mother's, met hers. She shook her head. "Why don't we throw a few while waiting for drinks?"

"The menus are here," Brenna said just as the waitress walked up again and passed out laminated booklets.

"If yer drinking, I recommend ye try at least a shot of the house whisky," the waitress said. "For the wee one, there's Club Orange."

"What's that?" Cassidy asked.

"It's a carbonated fruit drink," the waitress replied.

"Like soda?" The waitress nodded. "That's fine." Her son's drink arranged, Cassidy looked at the beer and wine list for herself. It seemed worthwhile to try the whisky, but she wasn't interested in that for an entire meal. "I'll have the Westport Blonde," she decided, seeing it described as light ale. "But I'd like to try the whisky, too."

Since James was sitting on Cassidy's other side, the waitress's expectant gaze turned to him. So did Brenna's. He said, "May I have a shot of the whisky, Mom?"

"You'll have soda with the meal," Brenna said. Her tone suggested it wasn't up for debate.

"Sure."

The waitress wrote on her pad. "All right."

Thomas said, "The soda sounds good. Do you have any other flavors?"

"There's also a lemon," the waitress replied.

"Fizzy lemonade," James interjected. "Sounds good, bro."

"Probably like a Sprite," Thomas guessed. He looked up at the waitress. Cassidy wasn't sure, but he seemed to be trying to extend his contact with her. He was smiling in the same inviting way he had when he was trying to divert Ryan from bothering her or Brenna in the kitchen.

The waitress was either oblivious, or uninterested. She replied, "Probably."

Thomas frowned and looked down at the table. "OK."

Brenna put aside her menu and before she could be asked she said, "Harp lager, please."

"Did you want to try the whisky?"

Brenna looked at Cassidy, then the boys. "All right. Just one shot."

When the waitress had left to get their drinks, the group looked at the menus for a long while. "Mom, are you really upset I want to try?" James asked.

Brenna looked up and exhaled. "No, it's fine. This is the safest way for you to try something. We're all here to watch out for you." Brenna bit her lip and Cassidy wondered what lie at the heart of the objection.

"There's a reason it's with parent permission," Cassidy said supportively. Brenna's shoulders relaxed at her words. "Alcohol isn't to be taken lightly."

"Yeah, okay."

When the whisky shots arrived, they lifted them in tandem. The waitress smiled. "Slainte."

James tried the toast. "Slawn-che." The waitress smiled at him. Thomas frowned, hiding it behind a sip from his glass of lemon soda. Cassidy bit her lip to avoid a chuckle and she saw Brenna doing the same.

The afternoon rain continued and dropped the temperatures upon their return to the cottage, trapping them inside long before sunset. They crowded around the small television set in a small living room filled with rocking chairs and a puffy pillowed couch, where the boys settled. The boys, used to remote controls, were stymied with the dials on the television, but eventually they found something that looked like a nature documentary. As the English-accented host, a stocky older man, began to discuss some of the sights, Cassidy excused herself to the kitchen.

Looking through the cabinets, she found baking cocoa and a tin of sugar. Stirring the two together in a saucepan, she slowly transformed the cocoa into warm chocolate. Gradually she added some milk. Stirring until it was hot, she turned off the gas burner.

"What're you doing?" Brenna had stepped into the kitchen.

"Making hot chocolate," Cassidy replied.

The woman's blue-gray eyes warmed from concern to pleasure. "I'll get the mugs."

"You okay?" Cassidy asked as she poured out the chocolate into the mugs Brenna set down.

"Yes, I think it's just this gloomy weather."

"You were off long before the weather changed."

"You mean at the bar."

"Yes. You really don't like the idea Thomas or James trying alcohol at home?" Cassidy explained her thinking. "My parents let my brother and me try different things when we were at home. It was always supervised. Drinking with them demystified it. For me at least." She was surprised to feel herself smile as she remembered sitting with her father on a fishing dock the summer before she went to college, sharing sips from his beer as they watched their bobs and waited for the carp to bite. That was a far cry from the angry, judgmental man he'd been toward her more recently.

Brenna bit her bottom lip but, again, when she spoke her tone was honest. "I have an uncle and a brother who are alcoholics."

"Oh."

"You couldn't have known." Brenna stepped closer and put her hand to Cassidy's elbow. "I know it should be fine. I think I just... I want to be there."

"You will."

"Not until late August."

Ah. "You won't miss anything. It's only a month."

"I'll miss all of you," Brenna replied.

Cassidy leaned over the two mugs she held out to Brenna and kissed her. "We'll miss you too."

The next day, they took the car into town, though it was only a mile, and explored the shops. James found his art gallery with the workshop and Brenna registered him. On a corkboard in the art gallery, Thomas found a flyer about a climbing group and, using the owner's phone at the next shop, he called the number. Brenna was anxious; he didn't have any of his own equipment. But the person on the other end of the phone said there was enough to go around. "Mom, can I?" he asked.

"What time's the climb and where?"

Thomas repeated her question into the phone. After listening a moment, he said to her, "In an hour. They're at the sport shop across the street."

"What will you do for lunch?" The climb would almost certainly go through midday. Brenna started into her bag for her wallet. "You'd better take something." She handed him a few of the bills she'd gotten at the Customs Exchange. "Hopefully it will be enough."

"I'll manage." He was practically bouncing, having obviously not expected to find one of his favorite pastimes on this trip. "Thanks, Mom." He kissed her cheek and ran out the shop.

"Can I help you find something?" The shop owner looked up from behind another counter at the sound of the door's bell when Thomas left.

Brenna looked back over her shoulder. Ryan was reaching for

something on a shelf and Cassidy had crouched to carefully oversee his examination of it. Their blonde heads were close and the woman was smiling tenderly at her son's excited description.

"Cass," she said.

The blonde lifted her gaze away from Ryan and found her. "Yes?"

"I was thinking of getting a Celtic knot?"

Her lover stood and walked over to her with Ryan holding an anthropomorphized sheep wearing a tartan sash and matching kilt.

Brenna pointed out the case of rings. "What do you think?"

"I think they're nice, but honestly, I'm more curious about the tartans," Cassidy said.

"What's yer clan name?" Cassidy and Brenna looked at the shop owner who looked up from some paperwork he was doing on the counter.

"I'm not Irish," Cassidy said. "But Brenna is."

When his gaze lit on her from over his glasses, Brenna supplied, "Lanigan."

"Let's have a look at the registry," he said, pulling out a large binder from under the counter. Flipping through he scanned several pages then finally stopped, finger resting on the page. "Yer people come from County Roscommon." She looked blankly at him. "Connacht province," he added. "Colors are spring green shot through with black, canary and white." He walked over to shelves stacked with an array of fabrics. Withdrawing two, he examined them more closely. Finally he turned to Brenna with one in his hand. "This is it. Clan Lanigan."

She took the patterned fabric in her hands with awe. Her family tartan. She tried to recall if she'd ever seen her father or uncles wearing this pattern. She's never seen them in kilts, but she thought her father had a coat, lumberjack style, that looked something like this. "What do you have available in this pattern?" she asked.

"I can order a few things made, or you can buy a bolt of the fabric to sew things yourself." He nodded toward the sheep in Ryan's hand. "However, I know we can make a new sash and kilt for your boy's toy there."

"How long would that take?" Cassidy put her hand on Brenna's shoulder. Brenna looked at her with surprise. "You don't think it would be cute?"

"I think it would be adorable," she replied, "but that will

probably take some time?" She looked back at the shop owner.

"How long are you here?"

"I'm here through the end of the week," Cassidy said. "But Brenna's here through the end of next month."

He glanced through his order book. "We could get an order through in three weeks?"

"Sounds perfect," Cassidy answered him then whispered to Brenna, "This is *our* family."

They decided Ryan would get the sheep as-is today, but Brenna would arrange for its new clothes. When Cassidy had taken Ryan outside, Brenna turned to the shop owner. "Can I also order a blanket, two scarves, and two ties?"

Writing it all down, the shop owner said, "Did you want any of this to take home with you today? We might have the ties."

She glanced at the rings again and shook her head at herself. Cassidy's decision to unite their family with this sort of gesture was a lot different than some sort of union that would be marked by exchanging rings.

"No, I'll come back after everyone's gone home and get everything at once."

Maybe by Christmas, she thought, she'd have a better idea.

She paid the custom order's deposit, then took the receipt and tucked it in her bag.

"Here's my card," he said, passing her one from a small tin by the register.

After reading it, she tucked it away in her wallet. "Thank you, Mr. O'Deas."

HANDLING THE HOLIDAYS

California
December 2001

BRENNA WAS grateful that she had chosen to wear only a decorative Christmas sweater and loose slacks. Entering the kindergarten classroom quickly reminded her of Ryan's fifth birthday party where she had first begun to see Cassidy in a different light. Though Cass was the one working longer hours filming a weekly television series she had become a "room mom" and was well known by the children in his class. She helped the teacher pass out the iced sugar cookies – brightly decorated with gel as trees, snowmen or snowflakes – and milk. The children called her "Miss Cass," and her abashed reaction came with the most adorable smile Brenna had ever seen.

Moving around to different tables, Brenna encouraged the children in their coloring and crafting. She was "Miss Brenna," because that was how the teacher had introduced her. But most of them didn't know her by sight. She was the one picking up Ryan in the afternoons.

Children's holiday music tunes floated from a boombox up at the front of the room. It sat on a chair next to a four-foot-tall artificial tree. The two of them, along with many other parents, had contributed boxes of decorative erasers, pencils, or sticker sheets, which the teacher had sorted and bagged, tying off each collection with a child's name on colorful ribbon. The children would open the bags on the last day of school before the holiday break, filling their school supply boxes with new materials that would be waiting for their return in January. The teacher had assured them that everyone would get one, but there was a noticeable effort by all of the children to be well-behaved.

Following getting their snacks, the children were seated and coloring gingerbread houses which would be hung on the hallway wall outside. Most were copying their names from their desk placards to "sign" the bottom of the paper. Brenna sat next to Ryan, who eagerly explained to her everything he and his friends at the same desk group were doing.

"Mikey's got a green crayon," Ryan said of the freckle-faced redhead to his right. "And he's coloring the tree outside his house." He picked up a crayon for himself. "I've got red so I can color the dots on my house."

The tree on Ryan's paper was already a whimsical mix of both light and dark green. Brenna decided he was trying to emulate her son, James, who often worked on his art at home while Ryan asked "what are you doing?" She seldom had to intervene. If Ryan's questions actually started to bother him, James picked his things up and moved into his bedroom, closing the door. Ryan had even learned to stop following him and would turn his attention to other toys.

"Dots? Aren't these gumdrops?" Brenna asked. The four of them–Cassidy, Ryan, Brenna and James–had put together a gingerbread house last weekend, and put red and purple gumdrops all along the roof line.

"Yes, but I want them all to be red," Ryan said. "Oriela's coloring purple on her doors and windows." Dark tight braids bobbing to the music, Oriela turned big brown eyes on Ryan when she heard her name.

As Ryan bent forward to do what he'd said, a lock of his hair fell into his face. Brenna absently started to brush it back. He put his crayon down and pushed her hand away.

"I got it." He pushed his own hair behind his ear.

"OK," Brenna said. He'd grown so much since starting kindergarten. They spent a lot of time together waiting for Cassidy to finish her work day filming a supporting role in a series. Brenna's own current project was voice overs for a cartoon series and had much shorter – and reliable – hours.

Sitting in a booth and listening for her cues in a headset was very different from full body acting, but she found it interesting. It also had tickled her when she saw some of the concept art and then the finished product: her character was an anthropomorphic tawny-colored cat.

Ryan's elbow bumped his carton of milk, which Brenna rescued before it could spill.

"How is everything over here?"

Brenna looked up to see Cassidy standing over them. "Hi," she said. "We're doing very well."

"Hi, Mom," Ryan said absently, still coloring.

"Does anyone need glue or glitter to finish their house?" Cassidy asked.

Oriela raised her hand. "Can I put glitter on the windows, please, Miss Cass?"

"Absolutely," Cassidy replied. "Here." She passed the girl a small glue stick. "Do you know what to do?"

"Glue where I want glitter, then shake," Oriela replied.

"That's right."

Brenna watched as the little girl carefully outlined each of her colored windows with the glue stick. When done, she shook the tiny vial of glitter over each. "Oriela, that's very nice," she complimented.

"Thank you," Oriela replied. "Thank you, Miss Cass." She handed back both the glue and the glitter.

Cassidy smiled as she received the items. "You're welcome."

Ryan finished coloring in his last gumdrop and sat back. Reaching for his milk, he said, "Done."

"That's very good, Ryan." Cassidy leaned over and kissed her son's head. Brenna inhaled the woman's scent as she came close to Brenna perched on a child-size seat. Discreetly, she cupped the back of Cassidy's knee next to her arm. Eyes smiled at her, then Cassidy said to the whole table, "We're about ready to line up for the assembly."

"Help me up?" Brenna asked. Cassidy's grip on her hand was soft and strong and... "Oh." She grimaced and rubbed at her lower back, stretching.

Walking a few steps away and leading Brenna to the side of the room, Cassidy said, "You looked like you were enjoying yourself.

Reminded me of you at the Halloween party last year."

"Yes. Circumstances changed. No Thomas" – he'd always been the bigger volunteer – "and no show stage to set up on."

"The haunted hayride we did with the kids this year was fun though," Cass said.

"Yes it was." Brenna remembered bouncing over the rutted path tucked among the hay with twenty of the camp kids, each of whom remembered Ryan and Cassidy from the climbing trip the previous year. Only one or two had remembered them from the Halloween party, but then again, everyone had been in costume.

She and Cass walked over to the teacher, Mrs. Henry, a young Black woman with a ready smile wearing a blue and white flower print dress. Mrs. Henry picked up a bright orange handbell from the corner of her desk and briefly shook it.

Every child in the room put down whatever was in their hands and brought their eyes to her. She turned off the boombox. "Good afternoon, class."

"Good afternoon, Mrs. Henry."

"It's time to clean our stations, and line up for our assembly. One-" she prompted lifting her finger.

"Clean up," they told her.

"Does everyone remember their job?" When all the children had nodded, she prompted, "Two?"

"Line up," the young voices chorused again, which made Brenna smile.

"All right. Let's clean up."

Standing back, Brenna marveled. Each child did a very specific task: gathering different craft supplies, paper plates, milk cartons, or picking up paper bits from the floor and throwing them away. Reusable items were returned to clearly marked shelves or put in labeled cubbies. Ryan's job apparently was pushing in the chairs while everyone else lined up along the wall by the door. When he was done, he took the last place in line.

The whole process took about two minutes and had been surprisingly quiet for all the level of activity. Brenna looked to the teacher as she noticed all the children doing the same, hands tucked together in front of them.

"Well done, everyone!" Mrs. Henry clapped and they set their hands to their sides. "Miss Cass and Miss Brenna will be walking with us. How do we walk?"

"In a line, one ahead, one behin'," the children chorused, the rhyme obviously part of how they remembered it.

Mrs. Henry said quietly, "Will you two please walk at the back? I will be leading the children."

"Of course," Brenna replied. Cassidy took her hand and they walked to the end of the line where Ryan beamed up at them.

"All right, children, follow me," Mrs. Henry's voice drew all their eyes forward and they walked to the cafetorium.

"That was such a cute program," Cassidy said as the three of them – Brenna, Ryan, and herself – entered her home. "I know they'd been rehearsing the songs and skits, but it was wonderful to see it come together."

"Your friend Gwen seems to have settled in nicely as a teacher's aide." Cassidy's neighbor worked at the school and they'd seen her in the cafetorium, assisting with keeping all the groups of children organized.

"Mm hmm," Cassidy replied, busy with Ryan's backpack, removing his calendar book with pages she would need to sign before Monday.

"Go play, Ryan," she said. "Just a few minutes. We're going to James' school next." After sending Ryan to his room, Cassidy led Brenna into her kitchen. "Want something? I know the kids ate all those snacks, but did you take anything?"

"I didn't. I'm not a fan of iced cookies."

"How about chocolate chip?" Cassidy replied, remembering she'd made a batch for including in Ryan's lunches. "Or do you think we should actually have a dinner? I know we're supposed to get out to the high school for the program there by seven."

James, Brenna's second son, was a junior in a high school near Brenna's home in Pacific Palisades. It was likely to be a long drive in traffic to make it on time.

"Leftovers or pick up something on the way?" Brenna replied.

"I don't have many leftovers here."

"Then on the way it is. We can get Ryan nuggets or a corndog, or something else easily handheld. And wraps for ourselves?"

"Do you need to change?" Cassidy asked. Brenna had a few things here, but it was rare she spent the night at Cassidy's home. More often they all spent the night at Brenna's home. There was more space in the four-bedroom house than Cassidy's little two-bedroom bungalow. They hadn't tackled the question of moving in together again since the argument when Cassidy had been recovering from the hospital. She just couldn't contemplate moving from this place, her first home since leaving college. And now there was another reason: Ryan had just started school.

Brenna shook her head. "I'm fine. I'll just tidy up in the bathroom."

"I'll get Ryan changed."

Cassidy watched Brenna step into her bedroom where there was an attached bathroom and shut the door. Quickly she went into Ryan's bedroom, selected and set out new clothes, still casual, but dressier than his school clothes which were, as usual, stained after a day in class.

His red shirt had been plain and necessary for his place as a "ball" in the Christmas tree arrangement by the choir director. All of the kindergartners had been stacked together on the risers, some wearing green – the tree – and others wearing red, or white – being the decorative balls.

But now he was going to be with them in the audience watching a short play, listening to music, and seeing James's and other students' holiday art projects. He'd done so well at Thomas's graduation and that had been half a year ago. While he put on his own clothes after putting his dirty ones in the hamper, Cassidy marveled at how much *life* had changed in just a few months, not just with Ryan, but with her and Brenna and the woman's two sons, as well. They had created new routines, and even for crowded nights like this, she found, they had an easy rapport and made decisions without a lot of conflict.

"I'm ready, Mommy," Ryan said.

She noticed that pulling his shirt off and the other on over his head had caused his hair to flyaway. "Let's brush your hair."

"And my teeth?"

"No, we're going to get food in the car on the way to the high school."

Ryan frowned. "We're going out again?"

"Yes. James has a piece in tonight's art show, but there's also a play and music."

"I'm tired, Mommy." Hearing the weak whine, Cassidy felt a pit of anxiety form in her stomach.

"It will take a while to drive there. You can nap in the car if you want, Ryan."

Cassidy looked over to see Brenna leaning on the frame of the bedroom door.

Ryan said, "OK."

"Good. Now, go brush your hair. I want to show your Mommy something, OK?"

Cassidy watched Ryan walk out to his bathroom in the hallway. Brenna took her hand. "What do you need to show me?"

Brenna smiled and squeezed her fingers. "I could see you getting worried, but I think he'll be all right. Anyway, I have something to give you."

"Christmas isn't for a couple weeks."

"It's not a Christmas gift," Brenna said. She led Cassidy into the bathroom. "Just something to make you smile."

Brenna moved behind Cassidy and nudged her forward into the bathroom. On the mirror in lipstick was the outline of a sizable heart, drawn in lipstick. When she glanced at the woman, she noticed it was the same color Brenna currently wore. "What is this?" She'd been spontaneous about this.

Cassidy looked again at the heart. The heart's size and position above the sink were both intentional, the heart surrounded her face.

"What this is, is 'I love you'," Brenna said as she hugged Cassidy from behind and pressed her lips to her cheek. Cassidy smiled, seeing the woman's lipstick had lightly transferred to her skin. Brenna said, "Now, you clean up while I see to Ryan."

James stood with a young woman at an usher point as Brenna, Cassidy, and Ryan approached the school's auditorium within the flow of other parents and family and friends of the performing students. "Hi Mom, Cass," he said. "How was Ryan's show?"

"Very nice," Brenna said. She inched toward him and he stepped back, a sign that he was not interested in a public display of affection. So she turned to the young woman, who had been to the house a few times in the last several weeks. "Good evening, Gail. Are you performing tonight?"

"Yes, ma'am." Gail dipped her head.

"I look forward to hearing you," Brenna said.

Gail handed Cassidy a program. "You can take seats inside anywhere you like."

"Thank you," Cassidy said.

"You'll show us to the artwork afterward?" Brenna asked James.

"Yeah. See you then."

She bit her lip but then nodded, not realizing until that moment that she had hoped James would sit with them. He was definitely more separated now that Thomas was out of the house and he did his own driving. Cassidy's hand around her squeezed lightly, drawing her gaze up. "Come on, let's find seats."

Nodding, she and Cassidy walked on either side of Ryan down the auditorium aisle and into a row of mostly full seats. They remained on the end in case Ryan's tired turned to tantrum. He had fallen asleep for a few minutes in the car, until they arrived at a drive through and collected him a box of chicken tenders. They sat parked for about five minutes near the drive through, so that she could eat about half her wrap. After kisses and napkins, and a few sips of iced tea, she had driven them the rest of the way to the high school.

Cassidy leaned over Ryan's head and whispered, "Bren?"

"Mm hmm?"

"You OK?"

"Yes, I'm fine." She exhaled and inhaled and sat up a bit straighter.

"It's a long day," Cassidy said. "We've been dealing with a lot of people."

"I know. I'm fine."

"Mommy, Brenna, quiet. The music people are starting."

Cassidy brushed Ryan's hair and kissed his head, then brushed her fingers across Brenna's shoulder before dropping her arm behind her son's head. "You're right, Ryan. Let's be quiet."

As the auditorium lights dimmed, signaling the official start, Cassidy's fingers again nudged Brenna's shoulder. "Go ahead." Brenna put her arm also along the back of Ryan's chair, resting atop Cassidy's. The contact did make her feel less at loose ends and they remained tucked around Ryan for the entire program.

Cassidy hefted Ryan into her arms when they stood at the end. Her son had squirmed, but the effort to remain quiet had exhausted him and he'd fallen sleep sitting up. He was nearly too big to carry and she had to adjust his weight on her hip several times before they emerged from the auditorium. She spied the art teacher–whom she and Bren knew from the art gallery where James went many days after school–standing next to a signboard that read "Winter Art Show."

While some did head directly to their cars, Cassidy noted that a sizable portion of those who had been in the audience walked down the ramp from the auditorium and right down the sidewalk and through the building door the art teacher held open.

"The students thank you for coming," she said. "You'll find some of them inside with their art. This way." The woman kept up a steady patter, mixing between the welcome and instructions. Several parents shook her hand and a few teens smiled at her. "Hey, Ms. Vetter!"

"Connie," Cassidy said as they approached. "How are you?"

"Doing well. Did you have a child in the performance?"

"James's girlfriend plays saxophone," Brenna said.

"That's very supportive of you."

"How is Micah? And Hannah?" Cassidy asked. They hadn't been to the gallery in a while.

"They're well. But at home tonight." When Cassidy moved to the side to let others pass them, Connie said, "Go on, Jamie's inside with the other kids waiting to show off his pieces." She did, however, tuck a hand lightly around Ryan's dangling foot. "Looks like you should hurry up. This one's already asleep."

"Can we catch up?" Cassidy asked. "Maybe stop by the gallery on Sunday?"

"It's football season. Hannah's a bit of a fanatic. But if you can make it Saturday, college ball is over for the moment."

"I think we can do that," Brenna said.

"Enjoy the exhibit," Connie said.

Cassidy followed Brenna into the corridor between all the different art classrooms. Hanging on the walls were paintings, sketches, and a few mixed media projects. By agreement they started on the wall to the right, walking along and looking at all the pieces until they came to an open doorway. The label on it said "Art Room 1-114." From an initial survey, Cassidy guessed this was the 3-D art class. There were pottery wheels and lots of tables for freehand clay work and it looked a bit like a class had just been interrupted in session. However, when she drew closer, she noticed the pieces were actually "on display" – sitting on boards with small a notecard laying on the corner, identifying the work and the student artist by name.

"This is the class I'm currently taking." She and Brenna turned to see James stepping into the room.

"Which ones are yours?" Brenna asked.

"Here," he said, directing them toward a table between a window and a wheel.

On it, Cassidy could see an oversized toadstool on a field of green. A figure of indeterminate sex, its head covered in a hat, was curled up underneath and held a book on their bent knees. Each part appeared to have been painstakingly detailed and painted after firing.

"I made each piece separately." He pointed to the melted seam points connecting each element to the rest. "It's sort of Wonderland, but I didn't want to make the reader Alice."

"It's wonderful, James," Brenna said. She looked several times between her son and his work and reached for his hand. He nodded, but kept his hands together. She took a digital camera from her purse instead and snapped a picture of him standing beside his art.

Just before Brenna's hand touched Cassidy's back, more parents and students started entering the room. She put her hand down and turned to James. "When will you be coming home tonight?"

"We're heading over to a friend's to celebrate. Then crashing," he said. "I'll come home this weekend."

She nodded. "Is there a parent somewhere?"

"Yes, Gail's mom and dad. I've given you their number."

"OK," she agreed. "See you tomorrow then?"

"Before Monday anyway."

Cassidy felt Brenna's hand on her back drop away, a sign of her anxiety. She decided to suggest a meetup. "We'll be visiting with Connie and Hannah. Perhaps we will see you there?"

James nodded at her then leaned forward and one-arm hugged his mother. "Maybe."

Brenna briefly tucked her head against her son's and then braced herself, straightened, and stepped back beside Cassidy. "All right. I think it's time to get someone home to sleep."

Cassidy pulled Ryan from the back seat of Brenna's car and resettled him on her shoulder. He hadn't awakened the entire drive home. Cutting the engine, Brenna grabbed her purse and followed mother and son up the stone walk to the front door of the house.

Once they were through the front door, Cassidy moved quickly off to Ryan's bedroom, down a small hallway to the left. Brenna settled in the living room on the small couch and looked around at the space. *Everything had changed here.* It always surprised her how quiet the room was when her most vivid memory of it was when it had been filled with Cassidy's friends and their castmates from *Time Trails*, all celebrating Ryan's fifth birthday.

Then she sighed. They could have had another big party. But she had missed his birthday this year. She had been delayed on the return after shooting in Ireland. She shivered, recalling all the nights, nearly a week, that she spent in a cramped hotel in Nova Scotia, surrounded by passengers from airliners all over the world that had been diverted after US airspace closed. She had gotten a phone call through to Cassidy on the US West Coast by the second day and been able to talk to Ryan and James who had been staying with Cassidy since schools were closed. Thomas, however, had already been delivered to his college. It took another two days to get access to a phone again to call him at his dormitory, using the number Cassidy had provided. Because of that, he'd been the one to call Cass to report when Brenna had finally gotten an open airline seat and would be returning to California the next day.

"What are you thinking about?" Cassidy joined Brenna on the couch.

"Hmm?" Brenna blinked and shook her head, shaking off her melancholy mood, recognizing it was probably a symptom of having been rebuffed twice tonight by her teenage son. That final one-armed hug had reminded her how much he was growing away from her. She smiled at Cassidy when the other woman grasped her hands and held them together in her own.

"Stay here tonight," Cassidy said. "I know we usually would go to your place, but James won't be home and Ryan's already asleep."

Brenna didn't answer immediately and her gaze unfocused as she considered the logistics. "The gallery is closer to this side of town," she said finally. "You still want to visit Connie and Hannah tomorrow?"

"We agreed to. And" – Cassidy cupped Brenna's hand before continuing – "I think you need it."

"I need it?"

"While I understand James' reluctance to be hugged as a teen thing, it's a limitation on how affectionate we can be around him. You dropped your hand from my back in the art room when others arrived."

Brenna swallowed back an immediate denial as she met Cassidy's eyes. "I'm sorry."

Cassidy shook her head and shifted her grip around Brenna's hands. "I'm not upset. But you and I both are more comfortable being affectionate around Connie and Hannah and their friends." She dipped her head. "I miss when we can't touch."

Turning her hands over so she could clasp Cassidy's instead, Brenna leaned forward and pressed her lips to knuckles and then gazed into her eyes before pressing another soft kiss to the corner of Cassidy's full lips. "So do I," she said when she pulled back to meet the other woman's blue gaze.

Cassidy lifted one hand from gripping Brenna's and cupped her cheek, indulging them both in a languorous caress from temple to chin. Not to be left out, Brenna lifted her left hand to Cassidy's cheek and mirrored the action. Touches to her fingers and jaw made her lips tingle, craving contact, so she kissed Cassidy as heat flooded her belly.

She felt like it had been weeks, not mere days since she and Cassidy had last made love. Reverently, she undid each of the buttons on Cassidy's blouse slowly, pressing her lips to the bared flesh a few inches lower each time. As she parted the front clasp bra, Brenna closed her eyes at the feel of Cassidy's fingers sliding into her hair. Keeping herself grounded, she gripped the fabric of Cassidy's shirt bunched at her waist and swirled her tongue around the tightening bud of Cassidy's nipple. The blonde's groans spurred her to more bold possession and she pushed her back, seized the nipple between her teeth, and crawled over Cass pressing their centers together through their remaining clothes.

"God, Bren." Cassidy's whisper warmed the hair on Brenna's head, and she sucked alternately soft then hard until Cassidy's hips rose and fell so erratically Brenna was in danger of falling to the floor. The thought made her chuckle, which made Cassidy groan deeper.

She slid up for kisses, and manipulated the now-tender nubs with her thumb. Cassidy cupped her face, then slid her hands down Brenna's front, mouth following. She licked and kissed Brenna's throat while unbuttoning her blouse and pulling and twisting at her more modestly endowed chest.

"Ca-ass," she stuttered as the woman's teeth pulled one nipple particularly taut. "God." Though she had thrown her head back to give Cassidy access, she now dropped it to press a kiss atop the woman's hair as she felt her center throbbing nearer and nearer to release.

"I want to be inside you when you come," Cassidy said. One hand still cupped the back of Brenna's neck. The other slid down between their bodies. Brenna held herself up and rocked her center against Cassidy's. Long fingers loosened Brenna's pants. She gasped at the feel of those soft tips against her swollen sex. "Bren, my god, you're soaked." Cassidy nibbled Brenna's breast while she caressed through her hair.

Then Cassidy curled her fingers around her sensitive clit. Brenna felt her arms shake and redoubled her efforts to hold herself up. She continued to press kisses to Cassidy's hair, inhaling the light scent of her perfume and shampoo lingering in the soft gold strands.

Her mouth parted around an "Oh!" when Cassidy slipped two fingers inside and began stroking deeply. Her sex throbbed in time with each thrust. Brenna's hips moved involuntarily now and short incoherent cries burst from her lips. "Ca-ass." The hand on the back of her neck moved into her hair and pushed Brenna's head until their lips could meet again.

Cassidy paused her kiss. "Time to move this behind closed doors. We wouldn't want to wake Ryan."

"Just a little, oh god." Brenna felt so close though; she closed her legs hoping to stop Cassidy's fingers from withdrawing. "Please."

Cassidy kissed her softly; Brenna kissed her back harder, hoping to entice her lover to continue right where they were. After another moment though, Brenna sighed and ended the kiss. Hand in hand they went to the master bedroom.

Closing her door, Cassidy turned to see Brenna removing the rest of her clothes. The dress pants from their outing to the high school fell in a pile to the floor. As Brenna stepped out of them, Cassidy's gaze dropped to the apex of Brenna's thighs, remembering the feeling of being deep inside her lover's wet heat.

She turned on her clock's radio hoping the noise would cover their sounds. Then she grasped Brenna around the waist. Recognizing the refrain of Madonna's 1980s hit "Crazy For You," she thought, *yeah, yeah, I really am.* Brenna's gaze, pupils blown, filled Cassidy with lust.

Finger pulling at Cassidy's pants, Brenna said, "Now can I say how incredible you make me feel?"

"As often as you want." Once Cassidy stepped free of her pants and undergarments with Brenna's help, they moved together onto the bed, pulling apart the cover and sheets and arranging the pillows into a lover's nest.

Brenna lay down and the woman's tawny hair spread across the stark white pillows. From her knees looking down to simply soak in the vision that was Brenna's body – and constantly returning to the woman's eyes – Cassidy stroked the woman from neck to hip.

"Mm hmm," Brenna hummed.

"What's that?" Cassidy teased, catching the tip of a nipple with a tight pinch. Brenna gasped. She soothed the pinch with her fingers lightly and shifted her hands across Brenna's waist, dipping her fingers in the woman's navel and squeezing her thighs. When Brenna writhed she lay herself flush against Brenna and grinded between her thighs. Brenna hummed in her ear and the heat and tingles generated by their skin's contact made her own center hot and wet.

Rising again and taking in every inch of her lover splayed before her, Cassidy stroked the inside of Brenna's thighs, parting them further. She loved seeing Brenna's dark heavy-lidded eyes and slightly parted lips, gazing at her hungrily. Slow measured breaths moved Brenna's chest as the woman sought to control her rising arousal. Holding her gaze, Cassidy drifted her fingers through the thin hairs covering Brenna's mound, the direct touch after so much near-touch made her hips jump erratically.

"So sensitive."

"Cass, please," Brenna said, her voice throaty and breathless.

"I did say I wanted to be inside you when you came." Cassidy moved her fingers almost lazily, circling Brenna's core, noticing it softening and growing wetter. Her touch retreated back to the wiry soft hairs. "You haven't come yet, have you?"

"No." Brenna squirmed. Her pupils were wide, the blue almost gone. "But I want to."

Cassidy bent forward and kissed Brenna leisurely. She continued her lazy touches, close but not dipping back inside. Not yet. The woman's arms encircled her shoulders and tugged Cassidy forward. When her own hard nipples brushed Brenna's, they both moaned. The sensation made Cassidy's groin spasm. She felt lazy, playful. Teasing. So she dragged one of Brenna's arms off her neck and pulled back, sitting up.

To her surprise, Brenna groaned in a surprisingly high pitch. The sound was brief, cut off almost before it was fully realized, but that was definitely a whine. It made Cassidy chuckle. *OK, so the tease is working.*

"Cass," Brenna pleaded. "I need you."

"Like this?" Cassidy pushed one finger inside, stroking softly. Brenna nodded and her eyes squeezed shut. "More?" Cassidy asked.

When Brenna nodded again, she added a second finger. The feel of Brenna's sex throbbing around her fingers was intoxicating. She bit her own lip to silence a moan and shifted as her own sex throbbed.

Brenna canted her hips. "More."

Laying her palm on Brenna's chest and feeling the thundering of her heart, Cassidy watched the woman's pulse twitching in her throat. She withdrew her two fingers and circled Brenna's sex in broad rolling moves, gathering more wetness on her knuckles and fingers. Then, tightly cupping her fingers together, she pushed the middle three inside, curling them up, then moved them in short quick strokes.

Groaning, Brenna pushed onto her elbows and rocked her hips on each of Cassidy's thrusts. Inner muscles seized Cassidy's fingers.

Moving her thumb across Brenna's clit, Cassidy felt her orgasm. Auburn head thrown back, the reds among the browns caught the light from the bedside lamp. Her back arched, hips rocked, and her thighs, those powerful thighs that climbed mountains and had walked miles of the Irish countryside that summer, closed hard on Cassidy's forearm. Grinning, Cassidy twisted her fingers and pushed deeper still.

"Cass!" Stifling her exultant cry, Brenna bit her own lip. "Ungh. Cass, I nee-"

Brenna reached for her. Understanding need for comfort and weight to hold her together, Cassidy covered Brenna from breast to hips, pulling her in tight with one arm. Brenna continued quivering, core throbbing around Cassidy's fingers.

Opening her eyes, Brenna took in the darkness of Cassidy's bedroom, not sure exactly what had awakened her. Cassidy's warm breath just barely caressed her neck so she guessed the blonde was still sleeping. Then she finally realized the radio was playing. A female musician was singing about wanting open kisses in the moonlight.

Light kisses moved along her spine, reminding her she and Cass had fallen asleep after lovemaking the night before, remaining naked. "Good morning," Cassidy murmured, still kissing her skin, though now moving out to her shoulder from her neck.

"Morning," Brenna said. "Did you set an alarm?"

"No, but when I turned it on last night, I think it reset." Cassidy's long arm moved over Brenna's shoulder and pulled their bodies flush together. Soft breasts were cool at first, but then warmed gradually against her back. She rolled over and kissed full lips, broadly palming hardening nipples, before she nudged Cassidy onto her back and sucked on them in earnest.

She rocked into the warmth and pressure of Cassidy's sex against her own. When she briefly pulled back, she smiled at blinking pale blue eyes before nibbling Cassidy's arched throat. When more wetness coated her belly, she slid down between Cassidy's legs, trailing kisses down her sternum, between her breasts, and across the soft plain of her belly, until she reached Cassidy's center. Cassidy's soft sounds encouraged Brenna to continue. Gently lacing their fingers, Brenna inhaled the sexy scent and applied her tongue in short wide strokes, coaxing out Cassidy's clit until she could thoroughly trace the tiny knot of nerves with the tip of her tongue.

The blonde's sounds became throatier and she tugged one hand free, then tangled it in Brenna's hair. "Bren–"

"Right here."

She rubbed her cheek against Cassidy's inner thigh then kissed her clit before sliding up. Hugging Cassidy's side, she curled two fingers inside her. She nibbled Cassidy's lips and then her throat and ear when the woman threw her head back. Muscles squeezed her fingers and she caressed with care as Cassidy's orgasm swept through her body and the blonde hummed.

When Cassidy curled into her, she hugged her shoulder and kissed her cheek. "OK?"

"Yeah." Cassidy's voice was throaty and breathless.

With Cassidy and Brenna's blessing, Ryan ran off with several other children when they arrived at the WeHo home of Connie and Hannah. Their hosts brought out a tray of drinks and simple crackers and cheese hors d'ouevres and the four of them settled in the living room.

"It's been a while," Hannah said, settling her generous frame into an upholstered leopard print armchair. "Connie said you enjoyed the art show?"

"Yes." Cassidy sipped her lemonade and enjoyed feeling Brenna lean against her shoulder where they sat together on a sleekly black leather couch. "Sorry we haven't been by the gallery in a while, but between..." She fell silent as she saw Hannah wave her hand and shake her head, the bounty of her ebony curls bouncing.

"No problem. School years are crazy. I only see Connie because we live together. She's gone with Micah to school before I'm ready to roll out of bed. And this year started out more unsettled than most."

"It did," Brenna said. Cassidy found her hand as they both reached for another cracker.

"You went to Ireland, didn't you?" Connie asked. "Did you enjoy it?"

Brenna rubbed Cassidy's shoulder as she sat up, which drew Cassidy to look over at her and see her widening smile as she pulled her lips away from her glass. "Yes. It was a lovely family trip before I had to work."

Connie asked, "You're Irish, aren't you?"

"Both parents, but they were born here."

"Still, a chance to put things in context, I'd imagine. What they got up to around the house, the food, the sayings," Connie suggested.

"And the ruggedness and plain speaking," Brenna added in agreement. She went for a cracker.

To prevent Brenna from needing to speak while she chewed, Cassidy asked Hannah, "You had a summer trip too, right? Didn't your family go upstate?"

"Yes, we did. We're doing a showing and sale for the artist's commune in January. It's their biggest source of income for the year."

Brenna cleared her mouth with another sip of drink. "Is it just art at the commune?" she asked.

"Painting, pottery, wood sculpture, some upcycled art pieces, too," Hannah said.

Connie added, "There's a performance group, too, and the artists all design the sets. Others in the community write the plays. They're usually the native teaching stories."

"That sounds fascinating," Cassidy said. "We have a friend—former coworker doing community playhouse in the hills."

"Maybe you'd like to visit some time?" Connie suggested.

"It might make for a nice winter trip," Brenna said, sounding thoughtful. "Thomas will be back in town."

"It's not southern California. There's snow," Cassidy pointed out.

"I know," Brenna replied with a laugh. "I did grow up in Michigan after all. But they might enjoy the change of scenery from the city."

"I didn't have as much in St. Louis. Thinking for a moment, Cassidy recalled, "I did spend a few winters during college in Colorado." She suddenly remembered her first female experience, at a ski lodge, and felt heat rise in her cheeks. Quickly she shook her head to clear it.

A light hand slipped over her arm. "What?" Of course, Brenna had noticed.

"I've told you the story before," Cassidy deferred.

Connie chuckled. "Well, now you must tell us," she said.

Cassidy tilted her head and bit her lip. "It's about a... well, me and a girl." She cupped her other hand around Brenna's, too, taking support.

"In college?" Hannah asked. Cassidy nodded. "So you were a college convert?"

"No, no, it was... we were drinking."

"And you were pretty sure you were straight."

"Well, yeah. I had men falling all over me everywhere." She sighed. "Still do."

"That doesn't mean beans, Cass," Connie said. "Societal expectations make a lot of people think they should... even if they aren't sure."

"You know we were both married before." Brenna spoke to Connie. "It's been about a year of adjustments."

"I was married," Hannah said. "Angel though he is, Micah isn't an immaculate conception." She chuckled.

Brenna asked, "Was that hard on him? When you first dated women?" Cassidy knew Brenna was thinking of their sons.

"He knew I'd been miserable as a wife, but there was never any doubt in his mind that I loved him. Connie wasn't the first woman I brought into his life after his father and I parted ways."

"When was that?" Cassidy asked.

"Almost ten years ago now. Connie and I have been together for just about five years."

"Six next June," Connie corrected.

"Right." Hannah reached across the space and took Connie's hand, smiling at her. "Met her at a Pride march."

Cassidy saw the comfortable connection of the two women and squeezed Brenna's hand before sitting back herself and simply interlacing their fingers. "We didn't do that this year."

"You don't have to," Connie said, "but there's really nothing like it for community."

"You've known you were gay all your life?" Brenna asked.

"More or less. I resisted expectations by simply never dating, at least one on one. I'd go on group dates from time to time, but even then... I didn't find anyone I liked enough to take time away from my art." When she glanced at Hannah, Cassidy saw the unspoken *until her* in the woman's devoted smile. "The best relationships are when you share something in common anyway."

Cassidy began to think about her history. "I think you're right."

The foursome was quiet for a moment. Then Connie asked, "So you've been together a year now?"

"Yes, Cass came to my home for Christmas last year," Brenna said. She bit her lip and glanced at Cassidy.

Recognizing she was supposed to decide how much detail to tell of that rough beginning, Cassidy looked at Hannah and Connie. "I had come out to my parents and it didn't go well."

"I sense that's an understatement," Hannah said. "Your face looks a little ashen just from the recollection."

Exhaling and hopefully improving her color, Cassidy reminded herself that was in the distant past. "It's over now."

"So you don't see your family?"

"Haven't talked with them since February," Cassidy said. "You know I was in a wheelchair when we first met."

Connie nodded. "They didn't do that, did they?"

"No. My ex did."

Hannah gave a low "damn," and shook her head. "So you have plans for this Christmas to mark the occasion?"

"My son Thomas is coming back into town from college. So we'll have everyone together," Brenna said. "I was thinking we needed to go somewhere."

"Are you comfortable with...rustic?" Hannah asked.

"I've done a lot of tent camping," Brenna said. "And Cass and Ryan recently joined us."

"Then you definitely should join us in NorCal."

"But it's December," Cassidy pointed out. "Snow?"

"There's no snow on the ground there at the moment. But we do have several stone and wood lodges and the yurts. With group sleeping and the central fires, I swear it will feel cozier than a hotel room."

"What are the dates?" Cassidy asked.

"We start on the solstice, the 21st," Connie said. "But you can come up on the 23rd if you'd rather not be caught up in the ritual dances and prayers."

"We're headed there for the full two weeks," Hannah said. "The 21st through the 2nd."

Cassidy looked at Brenna's face and saw curiosity and excitement lighting the woman's eyes. "We should check that everyone likes the idea."

"It might only be for a few days," Brenna said. "I can't imagine either James or Thomas objecting, especially if James can draw or paint?" She finished the question looking at Connie and Hannah.

"Absolutely, he'd be welcome," Connie said. "And what does Thomas like to do?"

"He's my climber, loves nature. He's studying ecology."

"I'm sure there will be many things that he'll find fascinating."

"Can we let you know?" Cassidy asked.

"Of course, you have my number, and I'll see Jamie in school."

Thomas arrived home the Saturday before Christmas, exhausted from finals and a cramped drive in a compact car with four other college students. He decided he needed more supplies if they were going to northern California, taking Brenna's SUV to the camping goods store. James and Ryan had finished up their school semester on the 21st and went with Thomas, telling their mothers they had "super-secret shopping" to do.

So Cassidy and Brenna found themselves alone at home. The already sorted camping gear sat in the garage where Thomas had left it. "We shouldn't go empty handed," Brenna said as they closed the door after watching the boys leave together in the SUV. "We should bake something."

Cassidy's suggestion of cookies had moved them to the kitchen, and Brenna's recipe box. Checking the pantry, they agreed on four recipes, one of which was actually a breakfast bar. After helping each other tie their aprons and sharing kisses, they started baking. Brenna had turned on the radio connected to the hi-fi stereo system in the living room and Christmas music was pulsing through the house.

A jazz rendition of "Little Drummer Boy" was playing and they were filling thumbprint cookies with fruit jam when the boys returned to the house. "Man, something smells great!" Thomas's voice reached them from the foyer.

"Welcome back," Brenna said. Putting down the jelly spoon,

she dusted her hands on her apron and held open her arms as Thomas entered. He hugged her as James moved around them and snapped up two of the finished thumbprint cookies. "Wait," Brenna protested. Her son handed one to Ryan who had stopped by his mother's legs.

"Sorry, Mom," he said, not sounding sorry at all, before biting into the cookie. Ryan did the same.

"Well, OK, but just those... two," Brenna trailed as she saw Thomas reach around her to take one for himself from the caramel oatmeal nut clusters. She swatted his arm. Sheepishly he shrugged his shoulders but kept chewing.

Cassidy chuckled. "I think the best we can hope for is they won't ruin their dinner."

Thomas perked up, "About that. We figured you'd be busy when we got back, so we grabbed dinner on the way."

"What did you eat?"

"Burgers," Ryan said.

She looked at Thomas. "Burgers?"

"And fries," he added.

Deciding that she didn't need to question the situation further, she asked instead, "Did you get all your shopping done?"

"Yep."

"Uh huh."

"Yes."

Cassidy's hands cupped Brenna's shoulders, and the blonde looking down at Ryan now looking up after answering Brenna's question. "Did you eat everything?"

"Yes, Mommy." His eyes, so like his mother's, crinkled as he smiled widely. Brenna knew she would be able to find out exactly what they bought if she prodded Ryan just a little more.

"OK." Cassidy stepped around her and nudged Ryan's shoulder. "Go brush your teeth and take a bath."

Thomas kissed Brenna's cheek. "Did you have a good day?"

"We kept busy."

"The stores were packed," Thomas said.

"Shopping the day before Christmas will do that," Cassidy said. "Did you have any trouble with Ryan?"

"Nope. He was good. School's been good for him. He's gotten a lot more patient."

Brenna lightly smacked the top of James's hand reaching for another cookie. "Go clean up. And pack. We'll do a few loads to wash stuff you"—she looked between them—"either of you, want to take."

Cassidy leaned on the counter watching the boys disappear into the bedroom wing down a hallway to the left of the living room. "So they took care of it. Hmm."

"Yours will eventually get there too," Brenna said. "Shall I see what we have for leftovers?"

"OK. I'll put this last batch in."

"All right."

Cassidy stepped out of the passenger seat of Brenna's SUV when they were parked at the end of what had turned out to be a long winding drive up to one of the lodge houses. They'd been traveling in deeply wooded areas for nearly an hour, at the end of a six-hour highway drive, stopping every couple hours to stretch their legs and let everyone go to the bathroom. The boys all piled out and groaned and stretched to varying degrees.

"Mommy!"

"Yes, Ryan?"

"Can I take Ranger to meet the other dogs?"

She looked where her son was pointing and saw a group of people moving around several tents and a large yurt on the far side of the cleared area. They had dogs around their feet and none seemed to be paying much attention to their group just arriving. The calm suggested there wasn't going to be any territorial behavior, and if there was something, there were several adults around to intervene.

"Yes. OK." Cassidy watched as the dalmatian trotted alongside Ryan, her son holding his leash wrapped halfway up his arm. "You should unwind a bit though."

The boy pulled the leash off his arm and it tangled into a couple knots. Cassidy sighed, but she did nothing. She just hoped Ranger wouldn't go tearing off after a rabbit and drag Ryan into the dirt.

"Ranger, look!" Ryan ran off. His shout had turned heads and Cassidy saw that Micah was among the people Ryan was running toward. "Hi, Micah!" Her son waved enthusiastically.

"Hi, Ry," Micah said. He lifted his head and waved at Cassidy. "Moms are inside."

Cassidy nodded, too drained to yell, and gathered up one of the food containers. "Bren, Micah says Connie and Hannah are inside." She felt the nip of the air and was glad they had insisted everyone put on a couple layers. Brenna was rolling up the sleeves of her red plaid shirt as she moved around to the back of the SUV. She studied the woman's auburn hair which had been tied back and pinned up, finding herself itching to get her fingers into it, dislodge the pins. She inhaled instead, deciding it must be the crisp air making her feel so vigorously alive.

"Alright." Brenna too, grabbed another food container. Thomas and James were off to the side talking and stretching. "We'll leave everything else here until we know where we can set up," she told them.

"OK." Thomas stopped stretching and moved quickly to his mother's side. "I like it."

"I'm glad you approve," Brenna said.

Inside the lodge was the layout of a one-room space, a kitchen counter and cabinets on one wall, looked to have a sink and a stove, and a refrigerator. Between that and the open space filled with all manner of chairs, stools, beanbags, and toys, was a preparation island. The door creaked as they opened it and entered.

"Bren, Cass, so good to see you!"

Brenna said, "Connie, I don't know if you remember my oldest son? Thomas. Thomas, this is Connie, Mrs. Vetter, James's art teacher."

"Hello." She shook his hand. "Your mother tells me you're studying ecology."

"Yeah. I just started though."

"Well, I think you'll find some of our sustainability projects here very interesting."

"I look forward to checking them out."

"So where will we put our things?" Cassidy asked.

"Tents and yurts are for sleeping. We prepare food and bathe here. Though some of our people do go to the river for a more natural experience."

"Sounds like a plan," Cassidy replied.

"I'll ask around for the best place to pitch, and James and I will set up," Thomas said.

"All right," Brenna said. She kissed his cheek. Turning to Cassidy, she held out her hand. "We should probably find Ryan and at least make sure Ranger hasn't dragged him off."

"You did bring your dog. That's great," Hannah said, exiting from a small door in the wall.

"Did your solstice ceremony go well?" Brenna asked.

"Very well, thank you," Connie said. "There are more stories around the fire tonight," she added.

"And we have cookies," Cassidy said, holding up her container and pointing to Brenna's.

"Well, let's get those right over here," Hannah said. "Sampling is very important." Her gaze twinkled merrily and Cassidy's smile widened.

After the sun went down, the temperature, which had only been in the high 50s in the afternoon, dropped into the 40s. Blankets were shared and everyone was encouraged to gather in the largest yurt where a fire had been set up. The heavy canvas walls reflected the fire's heat and Brenna now believed Hannah's comment that the place was cozier than a hotel room. Her sons had made new friends, sitting with a mixed group of teens a few feet away. The youngest children had been coaxed to sit at the feet of several older men and women. While they had blankets, Bren saw that Ryan shared his with Ranger, who was dozing even as he was being used as a pillow. Ryan's new friend, introduced over dinner as "Kicheena," sat beside him, rubbing Ranger's head.

Brenna was tucked against Cassidy, the taller woman's arm snug around Brenna's back. "How are you doing?" Cassidy lightly filtered her fingers through the ends of Brenna's hair, which she had taken great joy in helping let down when they'd been eating dinner at the lodge earlier.

"I'm good." The ground wasn't the most comfortable, but she figured she wasn't going to be there very long. She'd rolled the sleeves of her plaid overshirt down again and sat on a bit of the blanket in her jeans and ankle-high hiking boots. She had her hands wrapped around a mug filled with hot tea. "Are you sure you don't want some?"

Cassidy beside her was also in a long-sleeve plaid shirt dominated by blues. Her gray turtleneck underneath had been pulled up to her chin. "I'm warm enough, thanks." Cassidy's own hair, up in a ponytail while they had been traveling, had been loosed around her shoulders. Briefly Brenna turned her face into it, feeling the soft strands against her skin and inhaling the mix of sunshine and wood smoke that already clung to both of them. Peace and love filled her chest.

Someone in the space tapped a drum, drawing Brenna's gaze

away from her lover's beauty. The sound echoed though, and Brenna didn't find the drummer before a set of bells sounded. Then a flute. And a tambourine. Another different drum with a slightly lower sound. Each player, whoever they were, had played one note and then stopped. The fire was large, but its light didn't spread as widely as its warmth.

One of the older people by the fire, a woman with wizened skin and white hair tied back behind her shoulders, stood and spoke. "It is our tradition to tell our stories in the night, in the winter, when we are all together and the great bear sleeps. At this time we praise and thank the sun and the earth, our mother and our father, for giving us life."

Brenna smiled as she listened, images dancing behind her lids as she closed her eyes to focus on the almost lyrical words of the storyteller. The local children were pantomiming in parts, and Ryan followed his new friends eagerly.

She felt a light pressure on her hair and knew Cassidy had kissed her. Pulling back, she looked up and found her lover's eyes shining with the fire's light. Leaning forward, she set her cup aside and pressed her warmed hands against Cassidy's cheeks. "Hello," she said.

"Hi."

When their lips met tenderly, Brenna sighed into the kiss, feeling Cassidy do the same.

"Is Ryan asleep?" Cassidy looked up as Brenna entered their tent, bent over to make it inside the small space.

"Yes, Ranger's with him." Brenna looked around. "What have you done here?"

"Made one bag." She had zipped together their sleeping bags into one big one.

"I like it."

"Figured it would be warmer than sleeping alone."

"Certainly more fun," Brenna said, leaning forward and kissing Cassidy quickly.

Once they cuddled up inside, the thick lining immediately started radiating their heat back to them, making the interior toasty warm. Cassidy leaned over, resting on one elbow as her palm settled on Brenna's stomach. "This definitely brings back memories," she said, leaning forward and kissing Brenna slowly.

"We didn't share a sleeping bag." Brenna's hand slipped under her pajama top and settled against her back as they continued kissing.

"But we did share a kiss." It had been their first, well, their second. Their first had happened in the woods after a night by the fire just like this one, with stories and songs, and adults and children, and warm camaraderie. Cassidy moved her hand under Brenna's pajama top and she found the woman's heartbeat, enjoying the change in its tempo as she licked and nipped until Brenna granted her tongue entrance. "Mm hmm," she hummed.

"God," Brenna husked as Cassidy squeezed and pulled a taut nipple and moved her kisses to Brenna's throat.

She slid one leg over Brenna's, which did two things, provided more of her body's warmth and brought her own center against the woman's hip, giving her friction to rub against. Her core throbbed. Brenna turned onto her side which bent her knee upward.

Gazes locked together, both slipped their hands inside pajama bottoms and encountered wet warmth. Cassidy arched forward, blindly seeking Brenna's lips and they nipped and kissed while rubbing each other until a sought-after release stretched their bodies taut and they cried out into each other's mouths.

Christmas Day dawned with Ryan pulling at their tent zipper. "Mommy. Gotta go."

"You know where the bathroom is," Cassidy told him as she opened the zipper a short length and leaned out. He was bouncing from foot to foot. She pointed him toward the lodge building.

"Come on," he said, but he started running. Cassidy shivered as she fully registered the morning's chill and started to pull back inside when she felt something laid across her shoulders. Glancing back, she met Brenna's blue eyes and fingered the fabric, finding it was her plaid shirt from the day before. "Thanks."

"Merry Christmas," Brenna said, leaning forward and kissing her cheek. "Come on, I'll put coffee on if it isn't already."

Extricating herself from the tent, Cassidy straightened and took Brenna's hand, helping her step free of the small shelter. She continued to hold Brenna's hand as they walked to the lodge building. Stepping through the creaking door, Brenna headed to the kitchen counter while she headed for the bathroom, finding Ryan already washing his hands. "How about some juice?" she asked as he wiped his hands on his pajama top.

"We opening presents?" he asked.

"After a while. When Thomas and James are up."

"I can get them up."

"I know you can, but it's a holiday. We should let them sleep in."

"OK," he said, walking beside her to the counter where he climbed a stool and sat down. Brenna was just pouring two coffees, so Cassidy went to the refrigerator and pulled out one of the juice boxes they'd brought. With Brenna on his left, and Cassidy on his right, Ryan sipped his juice and they drank their coffee, indulging in a slow wake up in the quiet.

"Good morning." Connie Vetter's voice accompanied the squeak of the door to the lodge and all three turned on their stools.

"Good morning," Cassidy agreed. The art teacher was already dressed for the day, in mountain boots, corduroy pants, a turtleneck, and a sweatshirt, everything in shades of brown and tan. "There's coffee on the stove."

"Thank you. I'm having tea," she said, getting down a metal box and scooping out a spoonful of loose herbal leaves into a ceramic cup. She put a pot of water on the gas stove top and leaned back against the cabinets to look at them. "Hi again, Ryan. How are you today?"

"Breakfast," he said. "It's chewy," he added, holding up one of the breakfast bars they had packed for the trip.

"I love trail food," she said. "Is it good?"

"Mm hmm," he said. "My Brenna made it."

"Your Brenna?"

"Yes. She's my mom's but she's mine too."

"Ryan are you finished?" Cassidy felt her cheeks heat. When he nodded, she helped him down. "You can go back outside, but stay close. And"—she kissed his nose—"please don't wake up Thomas or James, OK?"

Once he was gone, Brenna said, "We haven't figured out exactly how to do this."

Connie shrugged. "It's cute, but it's also not necessary to tell them to use something specific. You might push where they don't want to go. Kids often do it just fine on their own."

"What does Micah call you?" Cassidy realized she'd never heard Hannah's son say any one particular thing to Connie.

"When I met Hannah, Micah was already in school, good with language, had figured out relationships. Had a dad, had a mom. Heard his mother call me her girlfriend and use my name. Out of the blue, he's looking for something he needs to get from his room before visiting his dad's, and he shouts, 'Connie, help'."

Cassidy flushed as she realized how Ryan had probably picked up his choice of names for Brenna. "I've referred to you as 'my Brenna' when I've talked to Ryan - but that's usually because I'm stopping myself from calling you 'my girlfriend'." She wrinkled her nose. "We aren't girls and I don't like the trite way it sounds." She pointed out, "I have used 'my partner,' but not often enough, I guess."

"I guess 'my Brenna' it is," Connie said, finishing with a chuckle.

THE PREMIERE

Los Angeles, California
May 2002

CASSIDY ENTERED the bedroom, dropping her car keys on the dresser by the door. She smiled at the auburn-haired woman standing in just bra and panties, hands on her hips, a look of frustration on her face. She looked at the bed, where Brenna was currently focused, and refrained from sighing.

She had hoped that delivering Ryan to Gwen for babysitting would have given Brenna ample time to finish getting ready. But apparently she hadn't decided on her outfit yet. Three dresses and two pantsuits, one green and one black, lay across the bed.

Though there weren't expected to be many cameras at the small independent film premiere tonight, Bren had been wracked with nerves. If they didn't need to drive to the theater within the hour, Cassidy would take her lover to bed to relieve her tension.

She smoothed down the front of her own dress. The film was Irish, so while kelly green was not a color Cassidy could wear well, the muted and natural juniper green complimented her blonde hair. Other than the deep v neckline, the cut and length of the dress also was more demure than daring.

She had chosen a lariat style necklace with small diamond inlays that nestled against her collarbones before plunging down her breastbone.

To distract Brenna from her anxiety, Cassidy pulled from her purse the last piece she'd brought for Brenna to wear. "Right or left lapel, do you think?"

The pin with fabric fashioned in a flat bow was actually a piece of Lanigan tartan they had discovered in a shop in Ireland on family vacation the previous summer, just before Brenna had filmed this independent movie. Cass had several of the pins made from a bolt of the fabric, as well as vests and sashes.

Brenna turned and her gaze went from worried to awestruck in the space of time it took for her to look over Cassidy and finally lock her gaze on the pin she currently held over her right breast. "The tartan?" Brenna questioned. "You want to wear it?"

"Yes, and I have yours, too."

Crossing the short space, Brenna lifted her hands to take the pin. Cassidy stroked her fingers over slender hips covered in a short nude satin camisole and shapewear. Brenna's gaze found hers. "Put it on?" Cassidy asked.

Lifting the lapel of Cassidy's blouse Brenna set the pin in place. Her fingertips drifted off the pin's fabric and down across Cassidy's breast. "It looks lovely on you."

Taking a moment to kiss her, Cassidy smirked when Brenna gave a needy little hum as they parted. She then stepped over to the bed and lifted several different pieces. "Wear the scalloped black lace jacket," she suggested, "over your dark green blouse and black slacks."

Brenna took the clothes and Cassidy gestured to herself. "It's less formal, but so is the event, really. Pants will suit you sitting on the stage to answer questions."

"Sitting on the stage?" Brenna wrinkled her nose. "But I'm—"

Cassidy cupped her face and kissed her again to quiet her doubts. "You are *not* too old for that." She raised her eyebrow when Brenna opened her mouth to say something else. "I had Jane check the venue. It's an old theater space. Close quarters and all fixed theater seats. There's about eighteen inches of stage jutting out from the screen wall and only about four feet in front of the first row."

"So we're sitting on the stage."

"*You're* sitting on the stage," she reminded. "I'm sitting in the audience." She was going strictly as Brenna's plus-one and planned to keep herself to the background. She hadn't yet figured out how that would work during their arrival. Unless she could be directed to a side door.

Brenna held the garments to her chest with one hand and brushed the tartan pin again. "They're going to know you're with me if we both wear them."

"I'm good with that," Cassidy said. "We've been old news since before we went to Ireland."

Brenna's eyes were shining and her lips held an almost shy smile. "We're not old news to me. Being with you makes me newly thankful every day."

Cassidy smiled and kissed the tear tracing down Brenna's cheek. Gently she rubbed and removed the remnants of her lipstick. Catching the woman's blue eyes still tinged with gray, she teased, "Now, put *on* your clothes on before all I want to do is take them *off*."

Just as Cassidy had hoped, her words made Brenna chuckle. Finally she sat down on the edge of the bed and pulled on her clothes.

Brenna studied her appearance in the vanity mirror as she applied her makeup. The scalloped edge on her lace jacket did soften the lines of her dark green satin blouse. The deep v showed off the skin between her breasts. She frowned at her freckles. Drifting her fingers across the skin, she considered concealer.

"Don't you dare," Cassidy said. Brenna jerked her head up to meet her lover's gaze in the mirror as the woman stood behind her. "I love your freckles," the blonde went on. "You are Irish and tonight, of all nights, everyone looking at you should know it."

Her lips brushed the edges of Brenna's carefully pinned up hair and her hands lightly squeezed Brenna's shoulders. Nodding, Brenna felt her lover's hand circle on her back. Taking a deeper breath, she accepted the reassurance and focused on finishing her eye shadow. The hint of azure with the smoke drew attention to the blue of her eyes.

Next, she set a pair of small diamond studs in her ears, which caught and refracted the light each time she turned her head.

Once she had blotted her lipstick and practiced her smile, she stood. Cassidy pinned the small tartan fabric pin to her blouse then smoothed her hands down Brenna's shoulders to her hands.

Hand in hand they walked together to a full-length mirror on the wall. Lit by a bright fluorescent bar, they assessed their full appearance for the cameras.

As she swept her gaze over them both, her throat thickened. Her swept up auburn hair and Cassidy's falls of gold both shimmered in the light. Brenna's slacks and blouse softly emphasized her slight figure and Cassidy's dress hugged her tall and lean body.

"You look beautiful," Brenna said softly. It still amazed her that this beauty—who had terrified her not so long ago—loved her. She squeezed Cassidy's fingers and met the pale blue of her eyes in their reflection.

"So do you." When Cassidy turned into her, Brenna turned, melding their lips in a soft and tender kiss.

The road in front of the small theater was only moderately crowded as Cassidy pulled up her compact to the last stop sign. Sunglass-clad security motioned for her to roll down the window. "We've got an event. The area in front of the theater's closed to vehicles."

"I have one of the special guests," she said quietly, nodding toward Brenna in the passenger seat.

"Names?"

"Brenna Lanigan," Brenna said.

He lifted his walkie-talkie and repeated her name to someone at the other end. After turning and looking toward the theater, he finally lowered the walkie and

nodded at Cassidy. "Valet will take your car. Turn here," he added, pointing to the right, which looked like it would take them behind the theater. "The cameras are set up out front."

Cassidy made the turn and a suited valet motioned for her to pull up in front of his stand in the middle of the street. "What's your name?"

"Hyland." She stepped out when he opened her door. On the other side, Brenna was helped out by another suited young man. Neither of them looked much older than Thomas, Brenna's older son who was off at college in New Mexico.

His gaze moved over a clipboard on the stand, then he frowned. "I don't see it."

"She's with me." Brenna's hand settled on Cassidy's elbow only a half-second after her words to the valet.

"Ma'am?" He looked a little flustered as he looked up.

"Brenna Lanigan. This is my partner, Cassidy Hyland."

He looked down the list again. Expression clearing, he looked up again. "Ms. Lanigan, you're expected out front. They've arranged for the three principles to take pictures and enter together."

"And me?" Cassidy asked.

"Walk with me?" Brenna said. "I couldn't have done this without you."

Cassidy looked from Brenna to the security officer who had a surprisingly blank expression. Turning her gaze back to Bren, she searched the other woman's expression, fell in love again with the soft blue of her eyes and the hesitant smile. Instead of kissing her as she wanted, she held out her hand. "All right."

Brenna beamed and slid her hand into Cassidy's.

As the cameras and shouting rose around them, Brenna felt like she walked in a bubble. Cassidy's thumb was stroking the back of her hand. A glance to the side and seeing Cassidy in profile made Brenna's breath catch.

She's so beautiful. Her gaze dropped to the small tartan pin and her heart swelled.

"Over here!" Cassidy and she turned toward this and many other requests to "look this way." Their gazes caught in passing, she straightened her shoulders at the buoyant support shining from her lover's eyes. A gentle squeeze and a head tilt reminded her others were watching and she reluctantly turned in that direction.

"Ms. Lanigan!"

She followed the direction of the shout and felt Cassidy start to release her hand. Quickly she glanced up. "Stay," she said.

After giving a small nod, Cassidy released her hand, but smiling, she stepped behind to Brenna's left and tucked her right arm around Brenna's back.

Brenna tucked her elbow over the soft hand on her hip and felt her own smile go wide enough to make her cheeks hurt. She looked up to Cassidy as flashes continued around them.

Morgan Scott, the film's leading man, wearing a dark red brocade vest and a suit that was a shade between green and black, walked over from the ropes. "Brenna," he said.

"Good evening, Morgan," she replied.

From Derry in Ireland, Morgan Scott spoke with a thick Irish brogue. He held open his hands to Brenna and then drew back, searching Brenna abruptly. "You don' have the dongle, do ya?" He laughed.

"Not tonight," she replied, affecting the accent she'd used for the film. "But yer not out o' the woods yet."

The young actor laughed and hugged Brenna. Then he stepped back. "I'd like you to meet my wife, Brigid."

A small brunette woman somewhere in her mid-30s stepped forward, looking elegant in a modest black gown.

"I thought, since we have pictures together that Brigid might want to stay with your..." He trailed off while

looking around. "I thought you were married? You spoke of Cass so frequently."

She bit her lip. "We're not married, Morgan. Cass*idy*," she stressed, "is my partner." She nodded toward the hand on her hip.

"You're..." He shook his head. "Never would have guessed, just thought you were a friend."

"Close friend," Cassidy said.

"I can see that." He smiled and shook Cassidy's free hand. "It's nice to meet you. My wife, Brigid, is not much for crushes and parties, so I asked if she could go inside to the reserved area ahead of everyone."

"Brigid," Cassidy said. Her gaze turning to the Irish woman, Brenna noted, was warm. "I agree we should leave them to their spotlight."

Brenna balked. "Cass?"

"I'll be inside," she said, squeezing Brenna's hand before stepping to create space between them. She gestured toward the entrance and looked at Brigid. "Shall we find our seats?"

Brigid nodded. "Thank you."

"Well, that's awkward," Morgan said.

"Why?"

"Because I was expecting to put her in the hands of a doddering old mun," he said. "But she's now with one of the most beautiful women I've ever seen." He looked at Brenna. "I never would have guessed."

"I hadn't either, until I worked with her – or rather more to the point, had some non-working time with her."

"I guess there really is a difference being on and off-camera."

"Exactly."

Brenna gestured toward where she could see the film's female lead, Laila McAllen, surrounded by reporters. "Shall we join Laila and get these cast photos out of the way?"

"Delighted." He held out his arm. She declined, though she walked beside him to the far side of the theater entrance where Laila McAllen stood amid more flash photography.

"Hey Lay, what up?"

"Morgan!" The two fell into an embrace and Morgan kissed Laila's cheek.

Stepping forward while the two were still embracing, Brenna asked Laila, "How was your flight over?"

"Bren!" She fell from Morgan's arms into Brenna's and hugged her tightly. "It was good. Mum was a bit blighted, so we're savin' the sightseein' fer after."

Several photographers caught their eye, lifting their cameras, and so they posed periodically while they talked.

Brenna smiled. The 24-year-old Ireland native had played the daughter of Brenna's character Danae Tavish in "Fenris and the Faerie Folke." The two had become close during the five weeks of filming and Laila insisted Brenna meet her mother.

"Is she here for your big night?" Brenna asked.

"I left her at the hotel sleepin'."

Morgan held out his arm. "I sent Brigid off with Bren's partner."

"Cass is here?" Laila looked excited.

Brenna remembered Laila's kind smile when she'd revealed her relationship. It had been late, nearly the end of a long day of filming, and she'd found a phone to make the call. But she had yet again gotten the answering machine. Yet again she had forgotten the many hours of time zone difference. She still couldn't wrap her head around it. All she'd known is she missed Cassidy fiercely.

Laila had been nothing but supportive and even gotten Brenna to a phone at a break time that *would* get through. That phone conversation had been one of the rare times she got to catch up with Cassidy and hear about what Ryan, Thomas, and James were all up to as the start of school had loomed.

She realized she should probably return the favor and have the young woman meet her family. "How long will you be in town?"

"The promotions department gave us the week here," Morgan said. "Then we'll do a morning show on the east coast before flying home."

"That's going to do wonders for distribution," Brenna praised.

"We could use some witchiness," Morgan said. "Why don' ye come 'long?"

"I'm actually in the middle of a project."

"Oh, so we'll see you onscreen again?" a reporter asked.

"No, I'm currently doing voice work," Brenna said. "Filmation. But the character's under wraps until the episodes debut. Sorry." She dipped her head but returned her attention to Laila. "What other projects are you planning?" she asked.

"I think I might have a recurring part in a series. I went to a call back just the day before flying out," Morgan said.

"Laila?" Brenna asked.

"A guest role on Midsomer Murders," she said.

"It's a start," she said.

She was just pulling back from Laila's hug when a man in a sport coat, graying hair around his temples, stepped up to them. The host of the theater walked up next. A spryly built man, he wore a cocoa-colored jacket and tie with a vermilion dress shirt and black denim pants. She was grateful for Cassidy's foresight in choosing her less formal attire.

"Ms. Lanigan. Mr. Scott. Miss McAllen. It's a pleasure to meet you."

"Thank you for hosting us," Morgan said, shaking his hand.

"Bronagh was a student of mine," he said in explanation. "I'm glad to see his work get spread a little wider."

Brenna nodded at the realization that their director, Bronagh Clarke, was the one with the L.A. connection.

"We're planning a formal Q-and-A inside the theater." He looked toward Laila and Brenna. "May I escort you inside?"

They paired off with Brenna going with Morgan and Laila walking ahead of them on their host's arm.

Entering the theater on Morgan's arm, Brenna was aware of the flow of bodies following them. A small group sat to the left and she recognized Cassidy and Brigid among several unidentified people, most of whom wore cream pant suits with vermilion stripes on the shoulders and legs. She realized they were theater staff and their VIP guests were receiving popcorn and drinks.

She caught Cassidy's eye as they passed down the aisle between the seats and smiled. The blonde lifted her popcorn and smiled back.

The room filled with raucous sound as the general public was allowed in behind them. When they reached the front row of seats, she looked back and up to see if she could spot anyone in the film room. The projector screen ahead was dark.

But a moment later, when they had reached the small ledge under the film screen, a beam of light curled out from a hole high in the wall and illuminated the screen with a static image of the film's title card. Written in fanciful script were the words "Fenris and The Faerie Folke."

Their director Bronagh emerged from a side door with a dark-haired man beside him.

"Laila, Morgan, Brenna," he said and shook her hand. He gestured to the man with dark hair and dark eyes next to him. "This is Martin Crowley, an executive with the American distributors."

"Nice to meet you Mr. Crowley," Brenna said. Laila and Morgan followed suit.

"Martin, please." He walked past them and sat down on the stage. "Shall we answer a few questions?"

A female photographer and a man with a video camera materialized out of the crowd of those beginning to find seats.

The host clapped Bronagh warmly on the shoulder. "It's a fun film," he said. The young director blushed, which told Brenna all she needed to know about how a "little Irish film" had garnered an American premiere, in Los Angeles no less.

A theater staffer ran up carrying a portable microphone and handed it to the host. "Thanks, Jen," he said. Then he turned on the microphone, causing feedback. The crowd silenced.

"Welcome, everyone," he said with some measure of gravitas, "to the premiere of 'Fenris and the Faerie Folke'."

The applause was polite. Once she, Laila and Morgan were settled on the stage, they were introduced and the questions began.

Brenna kept her gaze moving over the crowd. If she lingered when looking toward the reserve section, buoying herself with Cassidy's smile, she decided it was no more often than Morgan who sought out his wife's gaze frequently.

"A film filled with fantasy and magic, and based in lore. What do you say to criticism this is Tolkien lite?"

Brenna bit her lip. The question hadn't been asked of her, but she remembered watching the Fellowship of the Ring film's fever back in November. She hadn't thought about it, but despite its modern setting it had often had a very "old" feel.

Bronagh answered, "We based the story off a wonderful book by Dar Woods. Fenris's story does use bits of Celtic lore, which is about nature-power." He smiled and turned to look away from the reporter, over to her. "We found a wonderful embodiment of that in Brenna Lanigan, who portrayed our determined mum Danae."

Dipping her head to thank him, Brenna smiled. "Home and hearth have always been cornerstones of a good life, at least in my experience."

She looked toward the corner of the audience where Cassidy sat and willed as much love as possible across the distance, silently thanking her for her support and part in creating the family life she now lived. Cassidy's smile widened and she raised her hands to her mouth, then lowered them forward, blowing her a kiss.

"Next question?"

"That's interesting," another reporter segued. "I thought there was more of the Harry Potter stories influences here."

Brenna looked again at Cassidy, recalling the matinee showing of that film they had taken Ryan and James to in December. The reporter was right. But then it had been clear to Brenna at least that the Weasleys were meant to be similar to a boisterous Irish family.

"Did you have a question?" the theater host asked.

"For Mr. Scott?"

The young actor looked over and smiled at the female reporter. "Yes?"

"Did you see Fenris as an active hero or a reluctant one in pursuing his love?"

"Active, definitely. Did most of the stunts m'self. You'll see that."

Brenna resisted the urge to chuckle. The young reporter's face suggested she had been looking for a character-driven answer. But after a moment, the reporter said quietly, "Thank you," and sat back down.

"Next question?"

Cassidy looked over at Brenna as the film played out onscreen. She was glad they were allowed to sit together. After the actors had taken some questions, and the director and distributor offered some facts about the American distribution plan, the lights were lowered. Brenna and the two other actors were led to the same reserved seats where Cassidy sat with Morgan Scott's wife, Brigid.

Sitting next to the film's director, Laila McAllen, the young actress who played Brenna's daughter had an adoring look whenever she glanced toward Brenna and Cassidy.

Cassidy was certain that the ginger-haired young woman's gaze dropped to her hand on Brenna's where it rested on the arm of the chair between them. The young woman's face had split into an almost lovesick smile, something Cassidy would have associated with a teenager.

Smoothing her other hand over their joined grip, Cassidy smiled at the sparkling light from the screen dancing in Brenna's eyes. When Brenna, Laila, and Morgan had been led over to them, everyone shifted their seating so that each could sit next to their guest. She insisted to herself that holding Brenna's hand was just as natural as the male actor, Morgan Scott, holding his wife's hand.

Onscreen the climax was occurring. Cassidy winced at Brenna's onscreen death, trampled by the Death carriage horses. Danae Tavish had lost to the very faeries she had conjured to drive off Fenris Firth from marrying her daughter.

She squeezed Brenna's hand on the shared arm between their chairs. She leaned close, until her lips brushed Brenna's hair, and whispered, "You really were the bad guy. Did you enjoy being the villain?"

"Every villain believes herself to be the hero of her own story," Brenna responded quietly. "She didn't think this man was good enough for her daughter. Didn't want him to take her away."

Cassidy nodded; thinking that way as an antagonist gave an actor realistic motivations to back up their performance. "You definitely left Susan Jakes' heroics behind," she complimented.

Brenna's gaze met hers with a question perched in blue eyes, which she finally voiced. "Do you think it was good?"

"I do." She started to lean forward to kiss her cheek when microphone feedback sounded. Straightening she looked back to the front of the theater as the lights came up.

Applause that erupted through the theater as the credits rolled suggested that most everyone present had a positive reaction to the film.

The theater's host again stood at the front of the theater with the young director. Cassidy tried to recall his name as the host spoke. "So now you've all seen the work of these fine people, how about we have them come back for more questions."

Brenna stood and her hand started to slip from Cassidy's. "Hey," Cassidy said. Leaning close she gave her fingers another supportive squeeze before mouthing, "love you," and letting her go. In the aisle, Laila grasped Brenna's shoulders and hugged her with a big smile before indicating Brenna should walk ahead first.

When she emerged from the interior theater between Morgan and Laila, Brenna saw the concession counters in the lobby had been covered with trays of hors d'oeuvres and drinks, marked alcoholic and not. As she walked up to the counter determined to claim a small wine, she walked past clusters of guests and overheard several positive comments about the film.

"It's quite family-friendly." Turning toward the familiar male voice, she saw Terry Brown talking with Rachelle Cheron. So busy with the cameras and her castmates, she hadn't seen either of them before the show. Quickly she stepped past another guest and approached her friends to say thanks.

"It's so good of you to be here." She looked up into his dark brown eyes. He smiled and dipped his head and his presence filled her with warmth.

"Read the write up in Variety," Rachelle said. "You could've called, y'know?" The dark-skinned woman with Louisiana Cajun roots looked comfortable in a stretch black and brown striped dress that hugged her curves and showed off delicate shoulders.

"I was just telling Rachelle that I think my daughter would enjoy this." Terry wore a sport jacket not very different from their host, in dark brown, and a pair of black slacks.

"There are matinee shows," Brenna said. When she turned to Rachelle, the woman caught her around the shoulders with a hug. She'd almost forgotten how tactile her former costar could be.

"Rachelle? Terry?" Cassidy's voice drew Brenna out of the hug and around to see the blonde walking toward them. She carried two wines. She held one out to Brenna, who took both glasses, just before Rachelle enfolded Cassidy in a hug, too.

"Hey, how have you been?" she asked when they parted.

"Good," Cassidy answered, even as she was warmly hugged by Terry. "How's the playhouse going?" She held his gaze when they parted.

"We are finalizing our spring schedule," he said looking from Cassidy to Brenna. "Should either of you be interested?"

"What's on tap?" Slipping her hand into Cassidy's, Brenna leaned lightly against her lover's shoulder and watched Terry's enthusiasm light up his dark eyes, even though his voice remained steady and calm.

"We have planned a mini-festival of several one-acts to open the season in February, then it's several plays we collected from The Kitchen," he said, referring to a little place in WeHo called The Playwright's Kitchen. "A cozy mystery, an historical piece, a musical, and actually one that has some 'magic' to it," he said, nodding toward the theater they had all just exited.

"Bren!" Laila hurried over to their small group.

"Laila," Brenna said. "I'd like you to meet some friends. This is Rachelle Cheron, Terry Brown, and Cassidy Hyland."

"Cass?" Laila's smile beamed and Brenna remembered she hadn't had a chance to introduce them before the film.

"I should thank you again for your hospitality," she said. She then explained to everyone. "Laila and her mother kindly hosted me in their home several times since the family lives in Derry."

"Where the film was shot?" Terry asked. "You have a beautiful country," he complimented.

"Thank ye," Laila replied, cheeks gaining a rosy hue.

A reporter asked to speak with Laila and Brenna. After a couple questions, Brenna had sent the young woman to continue to answer his questions and returned to Cassidy, still talking with Rachelle and Terry.

"I can't remember being that young," Rachelle said, looking after the young actress.

Brenna pointed out, "You're not that much older."

"My child has aged me," Rachelle said, chuckling. "I swear she's into *everything* the second my back is turned. Her tumble class barely dents her energy."

"Perhaps she will be a gymnast," Cassidy said.

"And I'll support it," Rachelle agreed. "But right now, I could use a break." She laughed.

Conversation shifted to Rachelle sharing her latest project behind the camera. "Coordinating all the crews can be challenging. But I love the process, filming, editing..."

"You direct?" Laila asked, in a surprise reappearance at Brenna's elbow.

"Yes," Rachelle answered.

"That's so exciting."

Cassidy leaned into Brenna's ear. "You want something from the platters? I'm going to step away."

"Please don't go," Laila said quickly.

"Excuse me?" Cassidy asked.

"I just really wanted to talk to you," she said. "Meet you. Bren told me so little about you. All of you, really," she amended her statement and turned to include Rachelle and Terry. "I want to learn."

Brenna reached out for Laila's arm. "Tonight's about being social," she said. "Relax."

Laila took a deep breath.

"When you return to the States next time," Terry suggested when Laila said she'd really like to see a play at his playhouse.

"I'd like there to be a next time," Laila said. "Bronagh said he would help me meet some people."

"Well then, there you go," Brenna said.

Laila finished her drink and Cassidy thought she did look less like a frightened ingenue. "Thank you for spending time with me."

"You're quite welcome," Brenna said. "How are you getting to the hotel?"

Laila shook her head. "Not for a while yet. Bronagh invited me to the host's after-party. You should come too."

"Ryan's with a sitter," Brenna said. "We should get home."

She thought about the parties she had attended. Being a lone single woman was not her idea of 'safe'. Cassidy bit her lip. "Are you sure?"

"Don't you want to go home?" Brenna said. "Everyone's very nearly left."

"Laila, can you wait a minute?" Cassidy tugged Brenna's hand and walked with her toward a quiet corner.

"What's up?" Brenna asked. "I thought we could spend the rest of the night together since we're child-free?"

"It's a *Hollywood* after-party. She should have a reliable escort."

"She's going with the director."

Cassidy bit her lip. "He seems like a nice guy, but he's kinda blinded by the lights, too."

Brenna stepped back, and Cassidy could see her processing heavily. "Okay. Let me see if Morgan's going."

Cassidy leaned against the snack counter and watched Brenna return to Laila and take her over to Morgan, who was still talking with his wife and a female reporter.

A short exchange later, after hugging Laila, Morgan, and Morgan's wife, Brenna walked back to Cassidy. "Morgan will be Laila's escort to the party. And they have their own rental."

"Thank you."

Brenna took her hand gently and kissed Cassidy's cheek. Against her ear, she murmured, "Will you tell me what spooked you when we get home?"

Cassidy nodded and the two of them walked silently out of the theater and around to the valet to retrieve the car.

"I didn't ask you if you wanted to go," Cassidy said after they were driving from the theater district. "Laila and Morgan will probably make a lot of connections."

"Let them. I've got the connections I want," Brenna said with a laugh.

At a stop light, she leaned over and kissed Cassidy's cheek again. "Tell me on the drive home what happened."

"Probably no more than has happened to a lot of others," she said. "But I remember feeling like I didn't have a lot of safe choices. I knew absolutely no one. I was trying to break in and the general gist was... play or no chance."

Brenna's hand slid over hers on the console. "I had a few come-ons when I was first starting. I don't know, though. I wasn't really all that circumspect."

"So you slept with someone if you were asked?"

"It was the 'free love' 70s." Brenna's lips pursed and she frowned, but she also nodded, then she intertwined their fingers. "Everyone did it. I don't remember thinking of it as an expectation or a problem, just what was."

"Things are different now. It's a recognized problem."

"But it's not solved."

"More people looking out for the young ones. Maybe someday it will be," Cassidy said. She lifted their entwined hands and kissed Brenna's knuckles.

Cassidy walked up behind Brenna in the bedroom and slid her fingertips beneath the straps of the woman's bra, guiding them off her shoulders.

They had arrived back to the house and immediately retreated to the bedroom to get out of their dress clothes.

She kissed the freckled skin she'd noted at the beginning of the evening. "Beautiful," she murmured.

Brenna hummed and canted her head to the side, granting her better access. Sliding her hands down Brenna's sides, to her waist and then in front, crossing over her stomach, Cassidy eased her fingers inside the waistband of Brenna's slacks. Continuing to kiss Brenna's shoulder, she hummed and swayed as the other woman pressed her rear into the cradle of Cassidy's pelvis.

"I do recall you saying you'd like to get me out of these clothes," Brenna said throatily.

Cassidy nipped at the pulse throbbing there, and Brenna gasped. "I did say that, didn't I?"

"Mm hmm," Brenna murmured.

"But I don't have any expectations," Cassidy said.

"That's what makes it even better," Brenna replied. "We're doing this because we want to."

"Oh, I definitely agree there."

Pressing her hands against warm skin at last, Cassidy smoothed her palms over Brenna's belly. One hand moved up under the loose bra until she cupped Brenna's breast. She pushed the other down until Brenna's slacks slid to the floor. Gently she palmed the woman's underwear-covered sex.

"How's this?" she asked, massaging with both hands. Brenna gasped. The heat increased between her legs and Cassidy moaned into Brenna's shoulder.

"Ooh."

Chasing the heat with her fingers, she pinched Brenna's nipple and slid her other fingertips around fabric until she was able to press up inside. Brenna reached over her shoulder and grasped Cassidy's head. "Cass." Her breath sped up and her hips rocked.

While guiding them to the bed, Cassidy stripped all their remaining clothes. She crawled onto the bed. On her back, Brenna welcomed her, cradling her hips between her thighs. Warm strong arms slipped around her shoulders and fingers tangled in her hair.

Brenna hungrily took control of their kisses. Cassidy delighted in the feel of the woman's strong legs flexing around her hips.

Supporting herself on one elbow, Cassidy moved a free hand between their bodies. Brenna gasped when Cassidy's fingers found her clit and stroked it.

Nudging her knees under Brenna's thighs, she gradually lifted the woman's hips. Then she sat up, pressing her touch deeper before bending forward to press her lips against the delightful expanse of freckled skin. She nibbled in circles across both breasts until she reached the hard-as-coral nipples. Brenna keened and clutched at her more tightly. "God, Cass..."

Cassidy chuckled and licked until her fingers were squeezed

and soaked and Brenna weakly pushed her head away from her over-stimulated breasts.

Dropping to the mattress, Cassidy pulled Brenna into her body and caressed her back, kissing her hair and cheeks. She twined their legs together.

Gradually she saw the pulse slow in Brenna's throat. She caressed and untangled disarrayed locks. Brenna grasped her hand and brought it to her lips, slowing kissing each finger.

A moment later, Brenna rolled over and rose above Cassidy, legs straddling her thighs. Auburn hair tumbling around her flushed face, she was the most beautiful sight Cassidy had ever seen.

"What would you like?" Brenna asked. "What would make you feel good?"

She didn't want anything more than this, Cassidy realized. She slipped her hands around Brenna's waist, grasping her ass and holding her snugly. Their centers were so close, heat mingling. "This is perfect," she said. "You on me, like this."

"This is all?" Brenna asked. She palmed Cassidy's nipples. Gaze never leaving her face, she slowly pulled and pinched and twisted. When Cassidy helplessly arched her back, seeking more, Brenna asked, "Are you sure you don't need more?"

"God, Bren..." She closed her eyes. Brenna's lips pressed to her throat, then her lips, then her collarbone. Each kiss sent a spark through Cassidy's body and yes... God, yes... She needed, wanted more. Arching her back again, she was finally rewarded with the soft heat of Brenna's mouth tugging on her nipple. "Yes..."

Brenna's throaty chuckle reverberated through Cassidy's chest, as she laughed against her collarbone. Their centers came into firm contact and Cassidy groaned. She lifted her thighs around Brenna's hips, locking her ankles around the woman's back, and the other woman rocked against her.

"Cass, god..." Brenna breathed harshly against her ear. "I love feeling you like this." Her fingers skimmed down from Cassidy's breasts, across the plain of her belly. Brenna grasped Cassidy's thighs and then stroked through the damp hair covering her sex, finding her clit.

Sparks went off behind Cassidy's eyelids. "Ungh." she groaned as her pussy throbbed. "Bren."

"Mm hmm?" Brenna's fingertips teased her, setting off more tiny sparks that brought her closer and closer to orgasm.

When Cassidy's orgasm shook her, she clung to Brenna, who

kissed her hair and wrapped her up arms and bedsheets. Sleep dragged at Cassidy's limbs and their heated bodies merged. She murmured what she hoped was "I love you," though her voice sounded incoherent to her ears. She started to clear her throat.

"Sh." Brenna's lips moved against Cassidy's temple. "I love you, too."

About the Author

Lara Zielinsky has been writing Sapphic (les/bi) stories for 20+ years. Hundreds of her fanfic stories are available at the Academy of Bards, FFN, and AO3 for free (*penname: LZClotho*).

She's been writing original fiction since 2005. All her shorts, novellas, and novels have leading women who find romance and adventure, (self) acceptance, and loving, supportive partners. She's written contemporary, historical, adventure, and fantasy setting stories.

She lives for word games and gloats just a bit when she finds seven-letter ones. She thrives on her NY Times games in the mornings and watching *Jeopardy!* at night.

Recently, she started her own editing business, LZ Edits. When not editing, she can be found reading, writing, exercising her dog, bicycling with her spouse, or sleeping on the beach.

Website: www.larazbooks.com